From the Publisher: Maya   d a
vision-quest. Peering tho   :he
unfolding of western civ   n's
culture and knowledge.

On this long day of tales, the girl undergoes a series of initiations. She earns the Red Cloak, a symbol of power but also of responsibility for the future of the clan and of humanity. She has become a keeper of deep memory.

"Red Madder Root is a great read and an invaluable contribution to women's literature that provides hints about the "Old Ways" before women's knowledge of biological and spiritual experience was suppressed. It interweaves knowledge about female sexuality and the healing power of herbs into several reframed traditional "girls stories," while taking us on a journey towards resolution of our conscious and unconscious desires and conflicts. The overarching theme is one of positive transformation, even during the darkest of times." — Dr. Diane Hennacy MD, author of *The ESP Enigma: The Scientific Case for Psychic Phenomena.*

"Red Madder Root embodies the living tradition of Women's Wisdom. These are truly living stories. I can feel their teaching power; they bring me closer to myself in deepening ways as I read them.

"If you like hidden teachings, and still feel the dreamlike power of old stories, chances are you too will love this book. If you know that it is natural to grow in spirit, and you feel a call to embody those dimensions in your daily life and life-calling, chances are even better that you'll love this book. I have enjoyed every page of it."

—Judith Sanford, Cranio-Sacral therapist

RED MADDER ROOT

TALES OF INITIATION

A Novel of Fairytales and Forgotten Histories

Hilary Jacobson

Dana Williams

RosalindPress.com

Paperback version with black and white illustrations:
ISBN-13: 978-1-955746-04-5

Artwork © 2022 Ruta Ciutaite, Blue Rue Designs

Subject Headings:
Literature and Fiction, Fantasy, Shamanism, Fairy Tales, Historical Fantasy, Historical Fiction,
Women's Inspirational Fiction
Women's Folklore, Religion, and Spirituality in Fiction
Teens Girl's Folklore and Spirituality
1.1

DEDICATED

TO THE WOLVES AND THE BEES,

AND TO ALL THE MANY BEINGS,

AT RISK FROM HUMAN DOINGS.

CONTENTS

Acknowledgements

This book gradually grew, through inspiration and co-creation, into the small but dense work of fiction in your hands. To my dear friends, colleagues, and mentors who made this book possible, thank you all. A special thanks to Nathan Schauer, for decades of writerly coaching, and to Carley Biblin, for your timely suggestions that helped me write better fiction, and to my son Immanuel: you were still a teenager when you patiently sat with me and shared ideas and wisdom for this book. Thank you for your companionship and inspiration.

To Dana Williams, for our friendship and for your support and co-authorship, my deep gratitude.

To artist Ruta Ciutaite, it is a joy to see the stories reflected in your creations. Many thanks.

A large part of this book was written after the deaths of my parents, in 2007, and while my youngest child still lived at home. Grieving the loss of my parents and preparing for "empty nest" motivated me to write about what unites us across time and place—teachings, culture, legacy, love.

I would like to express my gratitude to Mr. David Littlewolf, who taught me about wolves and gave me permission to use our interviews and his stories for this book.

— Hilary Jacobson, 2022

Introduction: Red Madder Root

The red root of the madder plant has been used as a dye from prehistoric times to today, to impart beautiful shades of red to fabric, wool, and fur. Beyond its use as a dye, the root and the leaves are used medicinally. While this use is neglected in the West, in Traditional Chinese Medicine and Ayurvedic medicine, the red madder root holds an important place. It is used as a blood purifier, to open obstructed channels in organs such as the liver and kidneys. It is used for women's health concerns, especially to treat urinary tract infections, hasten a stalled childbirth, and to treat amenorrhea (absence of menstruation) as an emmenagogue. An *emmenagogue* is an herb, plant or food that "encourages" menstruation, either by stimulating the release of the blood or by increasing blood flow.

In medieval times, the Catholic Church forbade growing or using any plant that might cause the end of a pregnancy. The use of so-called *abortifacients* was severely punished. Emmenagogues are not meant to end an established pregnancy. Rather, their use just before and during the expected menstrual flow might possibly prevent a pregnancy from taking hold.

In a society in which women are sexually at the mercy of men and are subject to repeated pregnancies all throughout their lives, leading to childbirth exhaustion and to untimely death, the preventative use of a gentle emmenagogue such as red madder root may have saved the lives of millions of women and children.

The red madder root, because of its utility as a dye, was never banned or forbidden. The women who were initiated into the Old Ways could carry its use forward in a secretive and meaningful way. The red cloak, for instance of Red Riding Hood, may be understood as a symbol of this lineage. The centuries-old struggle to carry women's knowledge forward through changing times and changing cultures is at the heart of this book.

Foreword — by Dana Williams

In 1979, Hilary and I were young music students studying abroad in Europe. We met by chance, and our friendship began.

I remember our excursion to the Art Museum in Zurich. Walking along a corridor lined with statues from ancient Rome and Greece, we noticed three slender, white marble columns that were freestanding at the end of the hall. As we approached them, we grew aware of a feeling of peace and serenity that seemed to flow to us from those columns. The feeling was so palpable that neither of us wanted to leave their presence.

Something like this is waiting for you in the pages of this book: artifacts of a time long past, still alive and vibrating with lived experience, calling you to sense, remember, and know.

When my friend began working on these stories, exploring ways to combine history with archetypes, spiritual principles and traditional fairytales, she invited me to co-author her "project." It was a pleasure to help her, and I was truly sorry when she finished the novel but then decided not to publish, explaining that the book would not be understood by a wider audience. I am happy that she is releasing this novel now.

Today, in a world that is torn apart, and that promises the possible collapse of much that we hold dear, we find sustenance when we turn our attention to that which expands, uplifts and unites. Grandmother's tales remind us of transcendent realities but also of concrete values in the here and now. They restore us to a place of peace, calm, and understanding— and they set us on a path to healing, so that we can meet, with our heart and sense-of-self intact, whatever may be coming.

— Dana Williams, 2021

Preface, 2022 — by Hilary Jacobson

I began writing this book as a creative experiment in 2003. But after finishing the tales, in 2010, I put this book aside. I did not feel that the time was right to publish.

Last summer, 2021, was a dark time for the world. Where I live, a once-in-a-thousand-year drought is taking its toll. Farmers have no water for their crops. Forest fires burn from July to September.

On an August afternoon, the sky filled with smoke, I remembered this little book. Taking it from storage, I went to a nearby creek where, close to the water, the smoke was thin and I could breathe. As I turned the pages and became absorbed in the stories, I was overcome with emotion and began to cry. It was the most remarkable experience. I could hear my own clear voice from my past, speaking to me with confident surety, and telling me how and why we commit to live our best lives, even in the darkest times.

Suddenly, I felt that I remembered who I am.

In the hope that this book will be of value to others, I release it now with, to quote the Old Testament, "blessings of the breasts and the womb," for its tales have to do with the desire to sustain and nourish all life, even against all odds, and even when all seems lost. May this book find its readers, and may it uplift, inspire, comfort and give strength.

— Hilary Jacobson, 2022

Preface, 2009 — by Hilary Jacobson

You have probably heard that wolves and men hunted together in prehistoric times, but you may not have heard that wolves helped women as well. They were our first nannies. Because wolves protected and cared for our children, women had more time to forage for food. This was crucially important for our survival. In the northern climes of the last Ice Age, humans lived close to starvation for thousands of years. Wolves not only babysat our children, they also went with the women into the wild and protected them while they foraged for food.

Such teamwork was only possible because both species have so much in common. We both hunt alone and in groups, we live in clans and share our food with one another, form lifelong bonds, and care for our young. Wolf mothers even care for cubs that are not wolves, and humans do the same: we adopt young animals and raise them as part of our family.

Women's connection with wolves may have been more important than men's. Wolfgang M. Schleidt, an Austrian professor, writes that it was "woman the gatheress" rather than "man the hunter" who provided the majority of our food at the end of the last Ice Age. According to Schleidt, women could only accomplish this feat with the help of wolves.

I had been working on the Red Riding story when I stumbled upon Schleidt's article online. I was thrilled to learn about the historic bond between women and wolves. But the real adventure began a few hours later, when I ran into two actual full-grown wolves in front of the local market in the company of a taut, indigenous man named David Littlewolf.

We got to talking. Mr. Littlewolf explained he was trying to accustom the younger wolf to the sounds of traffic and to the comings and goings of strangers. He said that the older wolf, who sat perfectly still and unperturbed, was a large Russian type of wolf, and that his calm behavior was a teaching example to the younger wolf, who stood looking anxiously at the scene.

Over the next few weeks, I visited Mr. Littlewolf on his mountain property with my son and daughter. Sitting on rickety chairs in the sun, a hyena in its own enclosure to one side, wolves in a large open enclosure before us, he shared with me that he is a shaman from the Nez Perce tribe, that his parents put the psychedelic mushroom peyote in his beverages from early childhood on, and that he was adopted into a wolf family when he was five years old. He told me that some of the many wolves living on his property were the descendants of his original wolf family.

Mr. Littlewolf told me a lot about wolves' uses today, about their use in search and rescue missions, but also their clandestine use as assassins by our intelligence agencies. He emphasized, several times over, that he had never seen or heard of a healthy wolf causing harm to a human unless provoked, but that there are exceptions—extremely rare wolves that are born with a powerful killer drive.

Of course, one never knows if what one is told is true, but I can attest that several wolves live with Mr. Littlewolf at his property.

Prof. Schleidt, the author of the aforementioned article, kindly responded to my emails. I questioned him about Mr. Littlewolf's story. He said that while he could not confirm the truth of it, legend has it that in times long past, the First Peoples would place their young in the dens of wolf families so they might bond as one family.

Can you imagine how I felt at that moment?

I had been writing about a girl and a wolf when I came across an article about women partnering with wolves for thousands of years in prehistoric times. An hour later, I was standing in front of two live wolves and talking to a shaman who may have been adopted into a wolf family as a child.

Was it a sign? An Omen?

The modern part of my brain told me that it was only a coincidence, nothing more.

But on that day, I actually paused for a moment and imagined that the main characters in my book, Grandmother, Wolf and Girl, had somehow found a way to communicate with me. But what were they trying to say?

I do not know, and I'll never know for sure. But on that day, I reached a firm decision: I would do this. I would commit to write and complete this compilation of strange and wonderful stories called: *Red Madder Root.*

— Hilary Jacobson, June 2009

Wolf Song

If human memory is short, how far back does human forgetfulness go? I do not know, but those who keep our memories safe in stories and in songs tell us one of our earliest forgettings is our history with wolves.

They say that we first befriended wolves on the cold grassy plains of the north when four wolf pups tumbled down a hill. While wrestling and snarling with each other the way young wolves do, the pups did not even notice the human boy who stood quietly by, watching them play—until he laughed and joined in the game.

When the wolf mother appeared with a freshly killed rabbit in her jaws, she marveled at the furless boy whose sweet scent told her he was still a cub, and who played with her pups as though they were one family. She carried the rabbit toward the boy and shoved it at his mouth. From the moment that the boy set his tiny teeth to tear at the offered flesh, she looked at the boy as her own.

But when the boy's father returned and saw his son huddled asleep in the shade of a bush with the pups and their mother, he did not know what to do. Having just felled a small roe deer, he threw the carcass in their direction. Surely the wolf mother would take the roe and disappear into the bush with her pups. But an even larger wolf appeared from the bush and stood before the roe, coolly regarding the man who now reached for his spear. But a woman stepped close and touched his shoulder. She had been observing the scene from behind a tree. Though terrified at first, she had regained her calm spirit and she whispered to him now that their son was not in danger.

That winter, the clan shared meat with the wolves, and the wolves shared meat with the clan. The wolf pups sometimes slept in the cave near the boy, and the boy slept and played with the pups in their lair.

Both wolves and humans valued their new alliance. For when wolves and men were hunting together, the wolves would pull down a weak or ill reindeer that lagged behind the running herd, but the men would throw spears that felled the stronger reindeer running on ahead. And when women went into the wild to gather food for the clan, the wolves went along to protect them. They also stood guard for our children. The Wise Ones say that humans learned loyalty and altruism from wolves, for when a wolf is injured, the other wolves of the clan provide food until he recovers. But when a wolf is ill with an infectious disease, he will leave the pack voluntarily so as not to infect the others.

The more that wolves and humans bonded, the more we valued the help and protection of wolves. However, it turned out that wolves needed humans less than we needed them, and so, when the wolves moved on, following the herds to distant lands and leaving our settlements abruptly, we felt their absence.

One day, humans got an idea: we could raise wolves as our own. Noting where a pregnant wolf and her partner prepared a den for their pups, humans speared down the wolves and took the pups for themselves. The women fed the pups with their milk and raised them next to their own children as one family. Soon, humans found they could breed the wolves and make them even more useful: if the stronger hunter-wolves were mated, their offspring were eager to hunt and to kill: but mating the gentler wolves produced offspring that happily guarded the children and served as companions for the elderly.

Human memory is short. Later generations would assume that the animal-friends we now call dogs had always lived at their side. They forgot about our history with wolves, forgot how the wolves had helped us survive, forgot how we killed the mothers and stole the pups. They believed instead that wolves are evil: for a wolf might steal into a village at night and take a young goat or sheep, and in times of great hunger, a wolf might enter a village in the light of day and take a woman or child.

Tales of killer wolves were told as a warning to children, and we still tell such stories today. We've forgotten that dogs sometimes went wild and mated with wolves, introducing their exaggerated traits to the wolves' gene pool.

Listen: The Wise say that a true wolf will not harm a human unless provoked. Only rabid wolves, or wolves that are corrupted by dog-genes and born with a killer drive, will do so.

The wolves' memories are long. They have not forgotten we were once one family. Next time you hear the woeful lament of wolves, think about what the song means to them. And know, too, that the sad, howling song the wolves sing is not the *original* wolf song. It is not the lilting, yipping, colorful, lyrical lullaby that, long ago and in another age, was sung to calm and comfort both wolf and human pups alike, lulling them to sleep, assuring them that life is good and they were safe.

And finally, ask yourself this crucial question: what did we humans do with our deep forgettings? For nothing is lost completely.

Did we perhaps store our memories away in the tales that we tell our children? But in configurations barely recognizable? Did we dress them up in spooky symbols such as witches, giants, golden balls and magic mirrors?

Could it be that our forgotten memories, hidden deep within these tales, make children want to hear them?

For children want to know who we are, we humans.

They want to become full and whole.

They want the Initiations.

Our children want to hear and learn the Old Songs.

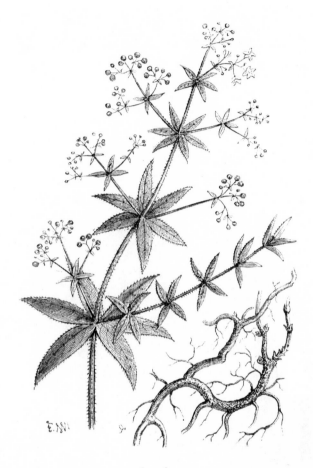

Red Madder Root
Rubia Tinctorum

Wolf, Girl and

Grandmother Song

Once upon a time, ages ago, a girl returned home much later at night than expected. As she slid beneath the bed covers, tired and looking forward to sleep, she was startled by a child's urgent whisper: "Sister, where have you been?"

"Shush! I will tell you tomorrow."

"Tell me now!" The child's toes pushed against her thighs.

"Stop, Carmona! Sleep calls! Listen: don't you hear it?"

The girl snuggled closer. "Mayana, please... I want to know where you've been?"

Mayana sighed. "Alright. I will tell you. I will tell you the story. But it must be short. Night swallows my words."

Mayana now began to tell of her visit to Grandmother, but soon she was asleep in the arms of her sister. See if you can tell the moment when her spoken story changes into a dream.

Mayana began:

I was doing my chores today when I heard a voice, speaking from inside me. It was Grandmother, saying she was in bed with a fever. She needed food and medicine brought to her right away.

Mother was busy in the garden, so I decided to go by myself. I packed food and water in a basket and pulled on a cloak that is dyed red with the root of the madder vine. Do you know why we wear a red cloak in the forest? It's so we will be seen as humans by the hunters and not shot at by mistake.

As I walked through the door, Mother called out to me: Be safe!

Keep to the path!

I answered: Don't worry about me!

First, I walked to the stinging-nettle: the cooked tops of nettle will build up Grandmother's strength. Then I pulled up some sticky mallows: their roots clear a wheezy chest. Then I foraged in the grass for plantains: their flowers make a tasty cough syrup and their leaves pull phlegm from the lungs.

The afternoon sun began to burn, so I rested in the shade of some trees, there where the *Teacher* lives—the sacred longflower plant.

Carmona, you know the lore: one longflower seed gives visions.

Two, and you sleep for hours.

More, and you fly into Deep Black Sky.

Visions, sleep, death . . .

I was resting, maybe sleeping, when I heard the longflower speak.

She said that something was forgotten, something I had to do... The *Teacher* told me to look deeper.

Look deeper... I jumped up onto my feet and searched hard through all my memories for the thing that was lost. Oh! It was Grandmother! She needed food and medicine brought to her right away!

I ran as fast as I could through the forest toward Grandmother's hut. I only stopped when I saw cattails growing tall in the creek, and went down to get some for Grandmother's soup.

Now, Carmona, mother has told us about a wolf who lives in the forest. He sleeps on a bed of dusty pine needles and old, cracked bones. He longs for the time when he was the friend of girls and women, when we made him scarves dyed red with the madder root so he would be recognized as part of the human family and not shot at by mistake. Mother says he is dangerous now to the human family who turned against him.

The wolf was already walking toward me as I looked up and saw him. Oh, Carmona! His massive head seemed to float in the wind, and his gray fur had a sheen in the sunlight. Then he stood before me on the bank of the creek, his large snout sniffing, checking.

But I was not afraid, Carmona! Not at all... not afraid at all... I wanted to play with the wolf, to touch his nose, to scratch behind his ears, to knead his fleshy neck.

And then—the forest went all quiet. The birds in the trees did not sing. The breeze did not blow. The insects did not buzz. The water in the creek did not flow.

Then the wolf spoke: "Little girl in red cloak, where are you going with your basket filled to the brim with food and flowers?"

"I am going to visit my Grandmother whose hut lies on the other side of the forest."

He walked closer to me on his silent paws. "Such a sweet girl. The day is growing old. You will get to Grandmother's hut much faster if you take the path directly through the forest." He pointed the way with his paw.

"Thank you for your help, Dear Wolf," I said, and ran off in the direction he pointed.

I reached the door and called out, "Grandmother, it's me, Mayana. May I come in?"

"Yes, come in, Dear. The door is open."

First, I cooked a pot of soup, using cattail, mallow, thyme, plantain and nettle. Then I carried the soup to Grandmother's bedside where I sat, balancing the steaming bowl on my knees. "Look what I've brought you, Grandmother."

"Yum, that smells delicious!"

I studied my beloved Grandmother, concerned about her illness. *Did she have a fever?* Her amber eyes glimmered, and her long pink tongue hung loosely out the side of her mouth between her large pointy teeth. I squinted and looked closer. Something was not right. One moment, I thought I saw Grandmother, smiling broadly, all her teeth shining. But the next, I saw a creature that was not unlike the wolf I had just met in the forest.

I asked, "Grandmother, why are your eyes so big today?"

The one in the bed said, "So I can better see your pretty face, my

Dear."

But I also heard Grandmother's voice answer from inside me. She said: "My eyes are your eyes! See! Perceive what is real!"

Still confused, I said, "Then tell me, Grandmother, why are your ears so big today?"

Again, I heard Grandmother's voice, sounding from inside me. She said: "My ears are your ears. Listen! Hear what is real!"

But the one in the bed said, "My ears are so big to better hear all your questions, my Dear."

"But then, Grandmother," I said, "why are your teeth so sharp and long, and why is your mouth so big today?"

Grandmother's voice inside me said: "Smile for the joy of the real!" But the one before me just grabbed at his belly and grimaced. "My mouth is so big—so I can swallow you whole!"

This was not Grandmother! I heaved the steaming soup at the creature and then ran as fast as I could out the door and down the path, heading for the forest.

But hearing the caw of a crow, I stopped. The bird had landed in a tree and was cocking its shiny black head and winking with its light brown eyes. It said, "Don't you want to tame the wolf? Don't you want to play with him?"

"Oh, no!" I said. "The wolf wants to eat me!"

I set off running again.

I only stopped when I heard a woodpecker drumming at me from a tree. He cocked his red head and drummed out, "Don't you want to be swallowed whole? You come out better than before!"

"Oh no! The wolf is dangerous and wants to eat me."

I was running again and calling out: "Help! Help! Help!"

I only stopped when I heard an owl hooting from a tree.

The owl said, "Nothing will come of it. Nothing will come!"

"Nothing will come?" I paused to consider what it would look like if nothing would come. For a moment, all was still. And then I saw a man, standing close by, leaning on an axe. I ran to him and pleaded, "Help me, sir! Please, help!" But he did not stir. He did not seem to see me. I set off running again.

Now I heard the wolf's paws, beating on the path behind me. He was quickly drawing close and would soon eat me, but a crow darted at his head, crying, "She is not ready to tame you yet!" Then a woodpecker drummed, "She does not want to be swallowed whole!" and an old owl hooted, "Nothing has come!"

"She's not ready!" called a strong, manly voice.

Hearing the sound of metal slicing air, I turned and saw the blunt side of the woodsman's axe catch the wolf on his shoulders and throw him from the path. I stopped, caught my breath, and watched as the woodsman walked to the wolf, went low on one knee, and then sliced open his belly with a dagger.

Grandmother rose up from the wound! She had been in the wolf's belly the whole time! She wore a nightgown and bonnet, and had not one tooth mark upon her. She stepped out of the wolf, bowed to the woodsman and said, "Thank you for your help."

"It was nothing."

Then Grandmother called my name and I ran into her arms. I hugged her again and again. "Oh, Grandmother! I thought you were the wolf! Or that the wolf was you! Oh, Grandmother, tell me, how was I to know the difference?"

"Is it really possible, Mayana, that you could not tell your very own Grandmother apart from the wolf?" She laughed and smiled broadly. Then she said, "Each girl must discover how to do this on her own. I had to find out, too. This is your first teaching. Know this, Mayana, and you are ready for the longflower seed."

Leaning close to my ear, she whispered, "The secret is this: you can befriend the wolf. Then, when he swallows you whole, you come out better than before."

Grandmother and I held hands and walked home through the forest.

The sun had set and the moon was swimming in a darkening pool of sky. The woodsman walked beside us, saying nothing, his axe in a sheath on his back. I looked up and studied Grandmother's face in the moonlight, studied all her features, noting exactly what she looked like: her eyes, her nose, her mouth. *I would not be fooled again.* My first task. The teaching. The longflower seed...

Mayana stirred in her sleep and felt Carmona's hand on her shoulder. It had only been a dream—the wolf, the birds, the chase.

She relaxed and settled again into her dream. Now she was dancing with Carmona and the young girls of the clan. They sang and skipped on a springtime meadow, sunny and warm. Their laughter was bright. But thunder rumbled above them in the clear sky. *What did it mean, thunder without clouds?*

Suddenly, darkness was all around, and it shuttered her senses. She could not see. She could not hear.

How was it possible that she could not see, could not hear? Slowly, her sight returned and she saw a throng of children running chaotically all about the meadow. Her hearing returned. She heard their screams, heard them calling to her to help them. *Help, Mayana! Help, help!* Her knees buckled and she fell to the ground and wept.

The thought came to her: *Might this be a dream?* Might she be asleep in her bed? She tried to awaken but could not. She tried again, but she only awakened again to this same place and to the unceasing screams of the children. To her horror, she realized she knew them, knew each of them by name. Knew all their stories. *Oh! The crushing knowing of their fates!*

Was it possible, she again asked herself, *that this was a dream*? She struggled again to awaken. Gathering all her will, she opened her eyes.

Mayana felt stone-heavy. Her face was damp. She pushed her fingers out from beneath the blankets and tested the air. It was chill. She saw that Mother was still asleep.

Mayana pulled tufts of wool from her hair as she left the bed. She squatted by the coals and layered them with dry leaves, twigs and small branches, and then watched as tiny flames took hold, waiting for the warmth to spread into the air of the hut.

Now Mayana stroked her mother's shoulder. "Awaken! The sun begins its journey. If you sleep longer, it will leave you behind." Her mother opened her eyes and pushed herself upright. Moments later she was heating water on the coals and warming finely ground bark and beaten seeds for breakfast. From outside, they could hear the movements of the clan. Soon Mother, Carmona and Mayana would join the women and children in the garden; the men would be away with the herds or hunting with the dogs. The smaller children would tend the young goats. The older children would help the elders with daily chores and mending. As they worked, they sang songs about each task, rhythmic songs of instruction that had been passed down through generations.

It was early spring, and clearing the soil for new growth was the main chore at hand. But, as Mayana worked, loosening the soil in long rows with a strong stick, she couldn't shake off a feeling that she should go back to the hut and check on Grandmother, who, she knew, would soon be heading back to her home, an hour's journey through the forest. She turned to her mother and asked permission to go to Grandmother.

Soon Mayana stood in the doorway of the hut, listening to Grandmother sing by the fire while wrapping cheese and paddies, nuts and dried berries in a fine leather cloth. Mayana stood for a while without speaking, as though sensing, perhaps for the first time fully, the older woman's importance to her life. Finally, she knew what she wanted to ask. She entered the hut and said, "Grandmother, there is much on my mind today. Do you have time for a story?"

Mayana's eyes were round and dark. In their depths, the solidity of her character intermingled with sparks of youthful curiosity. After her adventure with the wolf the day before, and her strange dreams that same morning, she seemed to see the world with new penetration—as if the world itself wanted her to look more keenly into it. She watched her grandmother, sensing the strength behind her likewise round, dark and deep eyes. She thought about the warm way that Grandmother's eyes shone when she spoke of times long past. Just now, however, the elderly woman's eyes were watchfully and coolly observing the girl, as if from a great distance. Mayana repeated, "It's been a while since you told me a story. There is still so much I do not know."

Her grandmother's eyes lit up. "Yes, Mayana. Let's go together to the Tree."

The Tree was older than the Elders could remember. It stood on a flat, grassy hill, below which the pastures and gardens of the settlement unfurled.

Its roots were large, they clasped to the earth like gnarly fingers, and its branches grew high and far to each side. Its original seed might have fallen into the crack of an immense grey boulder, and when the tree twisted itself out of this stone, rounds of rock split off around its base, which the people used as sitting stones.

The Tree had heard all the stories ever told—and so it was called the Story Tree. As a tale was told, the Tree would embrace it in its branches and make it part of itself, and at a later time, it might whisper the story back as the wind in its leaves. Most of the people could not decipher the tree's soft, rustling voice, but they believed that the long memory of the tree, and its quiet, patient urging, helped the storytellers recall all the details.

Grandmother and Mayana walked up the grassy slope, carrying flasks of water and provisions of food. Loping behind them came Fahrwa, the large half-wolf who was devoted to Grandmother. He was old now, his fur all grey and white. He moved slowly, with a limp, but he never let Grandmother travel alone. After greeting the Tree, they sat on the stones and rested. It was mid-morning. A breeze cooled their bare legs. Below, they saw the people of their settlement, busy with their tasks. Fahrwa sat quietly by Grandmother, his eyes closed, the tip of his tail sometimes tapping. "Now," Grandmother said, turning to Mayana. "Tell me, what is in your heart?"

Mayana felt pulled to look deeper into the scene before her. She saw Grandmother's thick silver hair, rolled about and upon her head, and her face, etched with lines like the sun-dried earth in need of a rainfall.

Mayana bowed her head out of respect for her grandmother. She began: "I want to talk about a dream that I had, Grandmother. It has been following me all morning like a hungry goat. I saw children, many girls and boys, all screaming and running and calling to me for help. What can it mean, Grandmother?"

Grandmother closed her eyes and said nothing, but the leaves on the tree stood out from the branches and three blackbirds alighted on a bough. Grandmother shifted her shoulders and sat tall. The motion made her seem stronger, younger, but her eyes were still closed and she still said nothing.

Mayana went on, "I also want to talk about..., about you, Grandmother, about the wolf, and about me. Why do such strange things happen? How could a wolf get into your hut? And into your bed? And how did you climb out of the wolf's stomach so healthy, whereas before you had been ill?"

Grandmother's eyes flew open. "What's this you say? Me, in a wolf's stomach?"

Fahrwa turned up his snout and whined.

Mayana scowled. She bowed her head and blushed deeply. "I see now—it was a dream. But it felt so real when I told it to Carmona last night. Somehow, in my mind, the story I told mixed together with my dreams. And this morning they both seemed true."

Grandmother said sternly, "It is not like you, Mayana, to confuse what is real with what is not."

Mayana was not used to this stern tone. She was shaken and surprised. But she looked up in time to see her grandmother's eyes soften.

"Why in the name of the Story Tree did you tell Carmona such a tale?" Grandmother asked.

Mayana thought for a moment. "She could not sleep because I returned home so late. You know how the little ones are. They want to know everything. And rather than tell her the truth—how I had been overcome by fear while walking alone through the forest to visit you, and how you'd then made soup for me instead of me for you, and then walked me home late at night, though you are not fully well—instead of telling her the truth, I made up a story."

"Mayana," Grandmother said, raising her fine hands and folding them before her heart, "tell me the story, exactly as you told it to Carmona. Tell it all, all the details."

Mayana began: "A girl was bringing her sick grandmother healing food and herbs. She left the path to pick the herbs and forgot the time. Then a wolf appeared and pointed the quickest way. But he must have run ahead of her, fooled the grandmother into letting him in, and so he ate her—he swallowed her whole. When the girl recognized the wolf in her grandmother's clothes, she ran away, but the wolf ran after her. He would have eaten her, but a woodsman stunned him with his axe, then cut open his stomach, and you appeared, Grandmother, you rose right out of the wolf's belly. You glowed with good health! Even your dress was whole! It was as if being in the wolf's stomach had healed you."

Grandmother stared thoughtfully into the distance, as though the story made her think of things long past, or as if she was reminded of another story. When she returned her attention to Mayana, she said, "Your dream of the children—it is a sign that you are meant to receive older stories, older songs. Mayana, give me your attention. Understand. Few may hear the stories I will tell you today. But those who have this dream should receive them.

"But the dream about the girl, the wolf and the grandmother concerns me. It fills me with questions."

Grandmother studied the girl, who now sat quietly, her spine in a gently upright position. Mayana was deepening her breath to heighten her attention, as she had been taught to do. Yes, the girl was skilled. She was advanced in the ways of healing. She had led the ceremonies of birth and death. But her teaching was not yet complete. And while her dream meant that she was ready for more stories, yet Grandmother suspected there remained matters of basic training that Mayana still needed to learn, essential matters that she should have been taught by the older girls when Mayana was little, but that, apparently, according to her dreams, she had not been shown. Perhaps the Story Tree will help me complete the teachings.

Now, you should know that in the time in which Grandmother and Mayana lived, all of the elderly women of the clan were revered as the grandmothers of all the people. Mayana and Grandmother were not blood related, yet Grandmother was Mayana's special grandmother because the Wise Ones had given them to each other as mentor and student when Mayana was two years old. Already then, Mayana was speaking to the spirits of the animals and following the voices of the plants.

The mentor-student tradition was old. It had begun in the time when Mayana's people lived far to the south, on the other side of the mountain range, close to the great water. There, on fertile land, many past generations had lived well. But one day, they were too many for the land to support; there was no longer enough food for all. Wisely, some of the younger men and women parted and traveled north, until they found another place to live that had plenty of water, fertile land and prey, and they built a new settlement. But again a time came when they were too many, and the young and strong moved on.

Now, many life-skills could be taken from one settlement to the next and taught to the young through remembered story and song, but the most ancient wisdom was kept only in the memories of those who were deemed to be Wise.

To carry this wisdom on, mentor-student bonds were formed. A mentor is different from an instructor. Where an instructor will teach a certain skill or area of knowledge to anyone able to learn, a mentor imparts an entire body of knowledge to one particular student over a span of many years. Mentors and students travel to be together as often as possible, sometimes a journey of days. When a student reached a certain age, they would go to live with their mentor's clan for as long as needed to complete their education.

Because Grandmother had already reached an ancient age when Mayana was born, and because Mayana's talents had marked her as a High Healer, she and her mother had moved to Grandmother's clan when Mayana was still a young child, so that Mayana might complete her education.

Mayana asked, "What are these stories, Grandmother? The ones you say I am ready to receive?"

"Oh, Mayana. They tell of times to come, times so far ahead that the mind spins to think about it. And they are true. The Wise have deemed them to be real. Very few can hear these stories, Mayana—because of the responsibility, and the sadness. So we wait for a sign."

Mayana was aware of being honored but also challenged. She sensed that this teaching would be different from any she had learned before.

Responsibility. Sadness. What could it mean?

Grandmother cleared her throat. She said, "Did you ever wonder how we find the stories that we tell? Why, for instance, you told Carmona a story about a little girl, a grandmother, and a wolf?"

Mayana's eyes narrowed with puzzlement.

Grandmother tipped her head to one side and smiled, playfully. "Do you recall the Grandmother Song?" She began to sing:

Come out, Great Mother,

show us your skirts.

Little girl is dancing,

Furry wolf is prancing.

Come out, Great Mother,

show us your skirts.

Little girl is ready for birth.

Fahrwa's tail drummed a gentle beat.

Mayana frowned. How could this be important? "I know that song," she said. "All the girls sing it."

"And well they should. It is the oldest of the Old Songs."

Grandmother leaned forward. "It tells of a time when wolves were women's friends, when they helped with the children and protected us in the wild. But it is also about the time of giving birth, and about the wolf in the body that gives birth."

Mayana frowned again. "I have helped in the birth ceremonies. I have not seen a wolf there."

"You have seen it, but you did not see it. The spirit of a wolf lives in your body, Mayana. Therefore, when a girl becomes a woman, she grows fur. And this is the challenge and the chance we are given: to befriend this spirit and discover the power of the wolf in our bodies. This spirit tells us who we are."

Mayana listened intently. Slowing her breath, she quieted her mind and absorbed the mysterious words. Grandmother went on.

"Every girl must meet this spirit in her body. The song says: the wolf prances. That means it wants attention. It wants to play. It wants to become your friend.

"Now, within the wolf is a girl. If you open the wolf's body, you will see her pink face. She is cloaked and hooded, well protected. If you part the folds of her cloak and touch her, she will rise. She will dance."

Mayana's eyes widened. Grandmother saw the sign of comprehension and continued.

"When I was a girl, our older sisters taught us the song and its ritual. We girls would sing it together when our fur grew. We would part the cloak and touch the girl and laugh. It was a celebration. The little girl inside the wolf!"

Mayana said, slowly, "I know the song, and have sung it with the girls. We also dance. But we do not laugh and touch ourselves." She sighed, still confused, but her curious mind pressed on: "What about Great Mother? How are we shown her skirts?"

"This takes more telling. In our language, the place inside the woman's body where the child grows is called the Great Mother, or the Birthing Mother. You cannot see the Great Mother; she lives in a hidden part of the body where it is dark as Great Night Sky. But when a woman is in the passion of her body, or in the throes of birth, the hem of Great Mother's skirt appears. The woman then feels that she wants to turn herself inside out, to give birth to Great Mother. Then the little girl cries with joy. She shows us who we are."

Mayana found this teaching new and strange. She said, "I know about the birth pushing joy. I have heard the women call out at night in the passion of the body. But I do not know about the Great Mother's skirts. Tell me, Grandmother, will I know this joy, too? Will Great Mother's skirts appear for me?"

So the girl had not yet been shown.

Grandmother said, "Mayana, this joy already belongs to you, for in your own dream you retold the Grandmother Song! The wolf is opened. Grandmother shows her skirts! Great Mother is enacting her birth!"

Mayana thought deeply. Did she really dream one of the Old Songs? She said, "Are all stories re-tellings of older stories, stories that we have not yet learned, or have forgotten?"

"Many are. But the Grandmother Song is the oldest. The health of the clan depends on it. It must be told and retold. If it is forgotten, it will appear again—as in your dream. For when a woman does not befriend the wolf of her body, its spirit possesses her. She then either shuts down and becomes ill, or she hurts others, calls names, lies, steals, and makes one trouble after another in the clan. And when all the women are mean or ill, there is no culture and no life worth preserving."

"I have known a woman like that in the healing hut," Mayana said, her voice trembling. "She is sick in her body but the healing plants cannot reach her. Her anger blocks their voices."

"Yes. It is just so. If a woman does not befriend her wolf, it plots revenge by spoiling her sight, closing her ears, and putting poison on her tongue. Then his teeth tear at her inner organs and devour her soul.

"I will tell you more now, Mayana. Listen: there is a ritual to the song. With your hands, you knead the wolf until he prances. Then you open the wolf's body and coax the little girl so that she dances. Then you pull at the skirts of the Great Mother. When she comes, you will know the joy.

"When I was little, we called this practice The Well of Birth, for it is a practice for birth, a practice to find the path of joy in birth. But it also keeps women well all their lives. The hardiest grandmothers still pull at Great Mother's skirts."

Mayana's eyes grew ever rounder and wide. "I haven't been told! I know the song—but I have not been shown the dance of the hands!"

Grandmother sighed. "It is a great work" she said, leaning forward and speaking so softly, "to keep the songs alive." Fahrwa at her feet whined, as if feeling the weight of Grandmother's meaning.

Mayana was concerned. Her grandmother would look frail at times, such as now, and then Mayana would remember how very old she was.

"But all people have stories in them," Grandmother went on, her voice stronger, "stories that tell how and why we live. Some dreams do this as well—such as the ones you had today. The Wise Ones know the children in your dreams, Mayana, know them each by name.

"I remember when I had that dream. I was younger than you are now. It was just before my own Grandmother passed and flew away. I told her about the children who called to me for help. She told me then that the dream is about changes in culture, about the loss of the teachings and a new way of life that brings cruelty and disaster. She told me that the Great Mother had chosen me to share her Sight, and then she told me the stories. Ever since that day, I have seen and known their lives as if they are my own. I have been waiting many years, Mayana, for one of my students to come to me with this dream."

Tree and Tower Songs—
To be Rooted in the Real

"Mayana, do you remember when you first learned the song Tree Grow?"

"Yes, Grandmother. I was so little! We girls would sing it, holding hands in a circle. At the end of the song we would stand perfectly still, with our eyes shut tight, to see who could be still the longest.

"We listened for a river, way down in our bellies. And we pretended that we were a tree. Our big sisters told us we were should be still, settle down, go inside ourselves, and listen, see it."

Mayana sang:

Water flow,
Tree grow,
Quiet now,
Quiet now,
I am a river

Her voice trailed into stillness. "But Grandmother, what has this song to do with the girls in my dream?"

Her mentor said, "There is a girl, Mayana, who must live in a tower built of stone. She must live in the tower so she can learn how to listen. She will practice Tree Grow.

But, Mayana, before I tell you her story, you must first understand all the ways that societies will change, and how her times are different from ours."

Grandmother proceeded to explain the future of the world to Mayana, starting just a few years after their own time. She used her hands and eyes to tell some parts of the story. She stood, sang and sometimes danced the meaning of others. Some parts were so dark that she could only transfer them mentally into Mayana's thoughts, in moments of deep, shared, stunned silence.

The story she told began with raiding between clans. It showed how stealing and enslaving would forever change human ways of life. She said, "Mayana, when no more land can be found to grow food for all the people, and food becomes scarce, the raids begin. Then the raids turn into battles, with the strongest men of one clan killing the strongest men of the other, and taking all the land, the women and the children for their own. You must understand that these men truly believe that they own the captured women, and own their children, because without a powerful man to claim them, they would just be taken captive by another man.

"The boys of this time will believe that men are born to fight each other. It will feel as natural to them as if they were actually born to do it. And soon the peoples in all the lands distrust one another. They forget that we were all one family."

Mayana nodded her understanding. It was terrible to imagine such a world, but she could follow Grandmother's telling of its evolution. But then Grandmother told another part of the story, a part that confused her.

"There will be a new kind of song, songs that are sung by the men, for the men. They celebrate killing and victory. But the Old Songs and women's healing ways with plants will be forbidden. For the men's minds are locked closed, only accepting what they can possess and rule. But they do not possess the knowledge of the Old Songs. So in the New Songs, they will call women of the Old Ways evil. They will call us witches."

Mayana's eyes filled with sadness. "Evil?"

Grandmother nodded, and went on telling the future history of humankind.

"In this long age the land will be in the possession of the men, and be passed from father to son. Men will take wives who are still children, whose fur is still soft and breasts are high and small, for as children, they are not able to oppose them. But because the land passes from father to son, the men want many sons, and so the girls will die young of childbirth exhaustion. They will no longer remember how to move the moon-blood with the sacred plants, so their pregnancies will hold, though they often bear sickly children.

"Not all is lost. When women come together in the market or on the fields, their talk is full of laughter and story. They hope to hear in each other's tales what is real about who they are, and to be reminded of their purpose and value. Sometimes, the Old Songs appear to them in their dreams, guiding and teaching.

"Life is off balance. For one hand needs the other, Mayana. Women and men, the two hands of the human, must hold together for all to be well. But in these times, the two hands are far apart.

"And so, when a drought befalls the lands, lasting ten generations, women's milk fails. Children are weak. Men have hardly enough strength to work the fields or to wield a weapon. Sickness pervades all the lands and many die.

"The Wise call this the Age of Darkness—for a dark belief will infect the minds of the people, teaching that an angry god is punishing them with weakness, illness, and death, because of something done by a woman, long before."

Mayana's dark eyes opened wide in shock. "Something a woman had done?"

Grandmother nodded. Mayana's attention to the details of the story pleased her. Fahrwa yawned and snapped his jaws. Grandmother patted his shoulder. "Just a while longer, old Friend," she said.

"Are you ready, Mayana? Close your eyes. Find your stillness. Practice Tree Grow. That's right. Find your calm. Listen."

And Grandmother went on to tell the story that we know as the Tale of Rapunzel.

A woman named Lyla, pregnant with her first child, will crave a certain thistle that is nowhere to be found, for the priests have forbidden the villagers from growing it. Lyla will remember her grandmother's words: that this thistle gives strength to women who are pregnant, and that it might yet still be found growing in a garden that belonged to a Woman of the Old Ways named Melinda.

The villagers rumored that Melinda was an evil witch who cast spells on those who came close to her garden, and so they feared her and stayed away. But Lyla, exhausted by pregnancy, thought: I simply must have that thistle! She begged her reluctant husband to kindly get it for her. Entering the garden at night, he tried to locate the thistle by his wife's description of it: the tall stalk, pointy leaves and spindly flowers. But Melinda could see the countryside all around from her high tower, even by starlight, and so she knew of his arrival. Throwing her old red madder root cloak about her shoulders, she went down to the garden and called out, "Who are you, hidden by darkness and stealing into my garden? What do you want?"

Cowering and trembling, the man said that it was all his wife's fault, for she had insisted that he steal the thistle.

To his surprise, the woman said that he might have the thistle, as much as he liked, and other herbs and vegetables as well, but under one condition: his wife must come herself and ask for them.

When the husband told his wife about this meeting, Lyla was

overcome by curiosity and agreed to travel with him to see Melinda.

Again from her high tower window, Melinda saw them approaching her gate, and she went down to greet them. To the woman she said, "Is it true that you sent your husband to steal from me?"

"Yes—but please. Understand. In the village, no one is allowed to grow plants that help a woman in my condition," and she pointed to her rounding belly. "Such plant lore is forbidden. The priests say women's herbs are the devil's work, because when Eve sinned and was thrown out of the garden, God cursed her and all her daughters with the punishment of suffering in childbirth. The priests say that any herb that makes pregnancy or childbearing less painful is against God's will. But surely, this cannot be true?"

Melinda listened but said nothing, so Lyla went on: "As for why I sent my husband—we hear terrifying stories about you and your garden! I did not know what kind of magical spell you might cast on me and on my unborn child. I only knew that I need this thistle!"

Now Melinda spoke: "Do you believe that God would put a precious child in your belly only to make childbirth a punishment? No. The priests tell you this nonsense to hide their ignorance. They have forgotten the lore, and rather than ask those of us who still remember, they declare that to use such herbs is a crime. It is as you say: the lore is gone from the gardens of the village. It is gone, almost, from memory. When I die, I do not know who will carry it on."

Lyla felt the pain of these words in her heart. She felt Melinda's sadness, her responsibility, as if such feelings were her own. There must be something I can do! she thought. And then she knew what it was. She said, "Melinda, if my child is a girl, I would like to give her to you as your apprentice, to be raised in the Old Ways."

Melinda started in surprise. "These things used to be arranged by the Elders. A mentor and student should share a similar disposition. Otherwise, the teachings will not be understood. They might even go wrong."

"But my daughter will surely take to the healing arts—under your tutelage," the woman argued. "Please, let us try!" And because Melinda very much needed an apprentice, she agreed.

Now, under Melinda's care, Lyla was brought packages of herbs and food by a "friend" who delivered them in the night. Her pregnancy went well and a baby girl was easily born. After childbirth, still other herbs were given to speed recovery and to bring about a strong milk supply. The healthy baby was well and seldom cried. Lyla named her daughter Rapunzel, meaning the root of the wild mustard in the old language. She hoped that Rapunzel would one day master the root wisdom of healing.

Up on the hill, beneath the Story Tree, Mayana opened her eyes and looked thoughtfully at her mentor. It struck her as unbelievable that a time might ever come when mentors such as her Grandmother would be rare, and have no apprentice. She herself had been given to Grandmother to be her student when still a young child. Her life had been planned out for her, just as it was being for Rapunzel.

Grandmother watched Mayana's thoughts, saw her unease grow, saw how she stretched her legs and moved her feet uneasily.

Then Mayana rose on shaky legs, turned away from the Tree and walked to a patch of sow-thistle. She nibbled on some blossoms, then bent off the stalks and sucked the milk from the stems.

Sow-thistle strengthens body and mind; it relieves fear, calms the heart.

Could it be true? Mayana thought. Would people one day no longer make use of such plants that grow freely and in abundance, all across the lands?

Sitting again on the stone, Mayana sipped water from her flask. She waited for the feel of wetness to spread soothingly through her body. Fahrwa, following her movements with his eyes, now looked to Grandmother, who gave him water in her hand before drinking herself.

"Grandmother, how does it happen?" Mayana broke the silence. "How is it possible that men and women forget to join hands and join strength? And how do the women lose our traditions?"

Grandmother seemed downcast as she considered how to teach this part of the story. Finally, she said, "Take heart. Nothing can be lost forever. It is all kept, even as these stories are kept, in the memories of the Wise. And when the Wise have all flown into Deep Black Sky, they are kept in the Memories of the Root, which is another name for Life. There, they can be discovered again by new generations.

"But as to how we will lose our traditions, Mayana, and men and women no longer join strength and work together... know this: as long as we continue to pass our knowledge from mentor to student, our way of life cannot be fully lost."

Grandmother now began to chant a song that Mayana sometimes heard the Elders sing at night, when they sat alone at the fire. It was called *Honor to the Root*. As Grandmother chanted, her hands rose in the air, dancing and forming patterns, carving out scenes. Her hands explained the meaning of the song. Then, like birds coming to rest, her hands settled onto her thighs again. She said: "A time will come, Mayana, when language can be read, when speech is pressed onto soft materials: clay, wax, bark, leaf, and leather. The bits and pieces will be gathered together into piles and bundles. They will be saved, copied, and shared. The knowledge held in the words now belongs to those who keep the images, and to those who can decipher them. Do you see? Hands no longer dance, songs no longer teach, knowledge is no longer a privilege to be earned and learned, told and treasured and passed on, from mentor to mentor."

Grandmother sank into herself, as if describing these things had tired her. Mayana waited. Grandmother, she knew, was now far away in her thoughts. Time passed slowly. But then, all at once, the girl was flooded with new energy, as if they had just sat down afresh to tell a new story, and Grandmother sat upright again.

She said, "The Wise have seen that far in the future, new ways of storing knowledge will open new ways of sharing for all people. But in the days of Melinda, it will control and limit what the people are allowed to know. Books that tell of our songs and healing ways are destroyed. The priests of the new dark belief no longer remember the ways that secured the health of humanity since our beginnings." Grandmother shook her head. "An apprentice needs years of training to become adept at medicine. To apply the knowledge is the work of a lifetime. But it will occur to men that they can take this knowledge from the Wise and press it into clay, so that only those men who can read the words can be deemed a healer, whether they have studied with a wise mentor from childhood on or not.

"But, Mayana, you ask how our traditions will slip away from us. How women will lose them. I will tell you. Far in our future, but long before Melinda's time, a man, the son of a great midwife-healer, will beg his mother to share her knowledge with him. He will take her words and give them to his friends. They will press the words into clay and say they are their own. This man will not reveal that his mother is the source of his knowledge; he will say that he himself is the author, and he will be called

'The Father of Medicine.'

"You see now how our knowledge is stolen from us? After that, Mayana, everything will change. For up until this time, it will be thought best to give birth to a child every four years—as we do now—leaving women time to recover from pregnancy.

"But this man will forbid all herbs that prevent pregnancy. For in his time, men believe they own their wives and own the babies in their wombs, and the men want many children for their lineage, even if this means that their wives die young from birth exhaustion. And so, these men will say it is against the law for any person to help a woman put four years between the births of her children."

Mayana said: "I understand your words. But why do women allow it to happen? Why do they allow their knowledge to be taken? Why don't they keep it for themselves?"

Grandmother frowned and shook her head from side to side. "The man's mother will give it to him freely. She hopes that her son's work will prevent women's knowledge from being lost altogether in the new times she knows are coming. She will not foresee the full consequences."

Mayana insisted, "But women can still pass their knowledge secretly, from mother to daughter, and mentor to student. What stops them?"

"Ah, Mayana," Grandmother whispered sadly, "some try. They travel north and live in settlements that are based on the Old Laws. For untold passings of years, they live as queens, priestesses, farmers, healers, musicians and poets. They teach their traditions to their daughters.

"But then, a new collection of powerful stories and songs reaches their lands. Men write these stories, and the men who bring the stories also bring new laws and new weapons. Now, women who follow the Old Ways are called witches and are punished.

"In Rapunzel's time," Grandmother spoke now in a stronger voice, picking up the pace, "Melinda is the only woman of the Old Ways for many days' travel all around. She has no daughters, because an illness when she was young prevents pregnancy. Her fields, gardens and pastures lie on a high plateau, and her home, built of sturdy stone with one tall tower, belongs to her alone—passed down from mother to daughter and from mentor to student through generations. And because the women of her line do not marry, the old property laws prevail."

Mayana thought she understood, yet she did not want to believe. Willing herself to hear the story to its end, she said, "Grandmother. Tell me what happens to Rapunzel."

Rapunzel was a healthy, ruddy-cheeked child with soft skin and clear eyes—thanks to the constant supply of Melinda's herbs and fresh foods. The other children of the village, who did not have the benefit of Melinda's care, were less healthy and therefore less attractive. In comparison to them, Rapunzel was indeed beautiful.

With each passing year, Rapunzel journeyed with her parents to see Melinda. They reminded her she would one day live and study with Melinda, and that Rapunzel could become a healer herself when she was all grown. But the girl never believed this story. She preferred the stories told by the girls of the village: stories that told of beautiful women who are rescued from lives of toil by rich Noblemen who love them for their virtue and their beauty. And that is why, before she slept each night, Rapunzel finished her prayers with the words: "Please, God, let me be beautiful so I can marry a rich man."

When Rapunzel was eight years old, her mother and father told her that the time had arrived and that she would now live with Melinda. During the journey there, Rapunzel was cranky and miserable. Her parents thought it was the chilly autumn weather that darkened her mood, but no—Rapunzel was simply angry.

She had been counting on the other story to be true, the glorious story that she ardently prayed for each night. She did not like this boring story about Melinda. She was also sad at leaving her little sister behind at the house: Susanne, four-years-old, and pretty as could be.

Melinda was waiting for them at the gate, wrapped in her cloak that was dyed red with the root of the madder vine. She greeted Rapunzel's parents, then smiled at the girl and led them into the house. Rapunzel, as always, thought Melinda looked old: she had a worn, lined face and long, white hair tied back in a braid. Yet, Melinda moved quickly and smoothly, not at all in the hesitant, awkward way that old people do, as she served them soup and bread, followed by platters of seed cakes and cups of sweet tea. When, later, Melinda showed Rapunzel to her own small room, the girl noted with satisfaction that the bed and covers were soft and fresh.

Back in the main hall again, Rapunzel's attention wandered to a large, arched door, slightly open, behind which was the tower. She could hear a soft, ringing hum, sounding from the shadows behind the door. Somehow, in all her many visits to Melinda's home, Rapunzel had never dared peek through the door into the darkness, though the door was often open.

Now Rapunzel's parents reminded her again that she was bringing honor to them and good fortune to all the lands. They enjoined her to pay close attention to Melinda's instructions and to faithfully attend to her duties. Her mother said, "We will visit you often with Susanne." Rapunzel's voice stuck in her throat. She wanted to say: *Do not leave me here!* But seeing the resolve on her parents' faces, she realized, for the first time fully, that this strange stone house was now to be her home.

At first, the days were endless and dull to Rapunzel, and she longed to be home again with her sister. But then flakes of snow began to fall, each day more, covering the trees and quieting the grounds, and she discovered to her surprise that she enjoyed the calm routines of life with Melinda. She also decided that she liked the food: seedcakes, small roasted birds and vegetable soup with chewy, dark bread for supper, and sweet gruels and baked apples for dinner. At the fall of dusk, it was cozy to sit with the old woman by the fire, and she liked the stories that Melinda told, about animals and plants. Rapunzel was not lazy. She worked hours each day for Melinda. As she faithfully followed the instructions and performed her various duties, she felt Melinda's pleasure and was glad. But, all the while, in the quiet of her heart, she dreamed on about marrying a Nobleman, and the prayer she spoke at night was still the same.

Melinda liked Rapunzel. There was so much she wanted to show her! Have patience, she reminded herself as, day by day and bit by bit, she began Rapunzel's training: how to plant and tend new seedlings, when to plant and when to harvest so that an herb's power is strongest; how to collect seeds and how to store them for next year's sowing; how to dry roots, leaves, and flowers.

The girl's book-learning was not neglected. She learned math and reading, and Melinda introduced her to the rules of agriculture and law— for these skills would be needed, should Rapunzel one day inherit Melinda's lands and take on the responsibility of being a mentor herself.

Four years passed and Rapunzel was twelve. Melinda was concerned, for it was long since time to teach the girl the hands-on art of healing. She had been watching for signs of readiness in the girl—simple acts of compassion or expressions of care for others—but they did not appear. The child was dutiful, yes. But something was missing. Melinda thought she knew what it might be—but how to remedy the lack? *These things should be taught to girl-children when they are very young.*

One evening, sitting together at the hearth, Melinda asked Rapunzel if she knew the Grandmother Song, and she sung it for her. The girl said that she had not heard the song before, and Melinda explained its meaning.

As Rapunzel listened, and understood, her cheeks flushed red. She did not know how to respond. She sat as still as if frozen, hardly breathing, and said nothing.

Melinda tried again. She asked Rapunzel if she knew the song called Flower and Cup and she sang: "Put a flower in a cup: it unfolds and opens up." But again, the child did not seem to understand what it was all about.

Melinda explained that this song, too, was one of the oldest songs. She smiled to herself, remembering how her own sister had taught her these songs—just as it should be taught, older girl to younger girl. She asked Rapunzel, "Were you ever shown how to find joy in your body?"

Rapunzel turned red with anger and said: "This is a trick, to make me touch myself where it is forbidden! I will be impure, and unworthy of a husband!"

The girl's response surprised Melinda, but she replied, calmly, that the Old Songs keep women strong and well, and that Rapunzel should not be angry or afraid.

Rapunzel could not agree. The girls in the village had told her never to touch herself there. Yet, as she listened to Melinda's words, she felt reassured by the steadiness of her voice. She couldn't help feeling that behind the songs, as strange as they might seem, was an intention to teach her something of importance, something that would help her feel better. So she said, "Tell me about Flower and Cup?"

Melinda explained: "Your rounded hand is a cup. It fits over your flower. Hold your hand over your flower, ever so softly, hardly touching, each night before you go to sleep. Imagine that the cup of your hand is filled with warm liquid that bathes and soothes the flower. As you hold your hand there, doing nothing at all, the flower will feel the warmth and will begin, ever so slowly, to unfold. Feel how it changes. At first, the change is subtle. Later, it is more apparent. That is all. Just a warming. That is the whole practice. But, Rapunzel, if the flower is not ready, it will not open, and that is fine. You must be patient. When it is ready, you will know it."

Rapunzel was relieved. What Melinda asked her to do was not impossible, for she would not actually need to touch herself. She decided to try, each night in bed, to practice Flower in a Cup. Weeks passed before she felt some subtle changes. Finally, she felt the changes so strongly that she spoke to Melinda about it again. She asked to know what happens after the flower warms and opens up. The old woman replied that when the flower opens, she should softly, gently, and playfully sing the Grandmother Song and do the dance of the hands. More time passed, and then Rapunzel came to Melinda again to ask another question: "Once begun, do the song and the dance ever end?"

Melinda smiled at the question, but noted the serious concern on the girl's face. She said, "The joy is always there to find, for it is yours, your own. But you can stop the dance and let the flower close if you should want or need to close it."

The girl looked relieved. Melinda said, "This is not the last of the Old Songs, Rapunzel. It is just where the teaching begins."

The girl's eyes lit up. "Am I ready to learn more songs now? What comes next?"

"The next song," Melinda said, "is Tree Grow." She sang:

Water flow,
Tree grow,
Quiet now,
Quiet now,
I am a river.

Rapunzel listened, finding the words mysterious. She asked about its meaning. Melinda then explained that within the flower is a force. Sometimes it is called 'Sleeping Grandmother,' and sometimes, 'Your Own Wolf.' When you give it your calm attention, it awakens. Like a spring of water, it starts with a trickle, then a gush, and finally it flows strong like a river. By the river grows a tree. It drinks from the water.

"Child. To do the practice, sit or stand quietly. Hold your arms upwards or stretched in front of you as though you are the tree. Sing the song softly and then listen inside to the base of your belly, where the spring begins and the river flows. Become the tree calmly growing by your river."

In the days that followed, Rapunzel sang Tree Grow and tried to follow the instructions. But when she was alone, she often felt drawn to sing and play the Grandmother Song instead. Perhaps she was not yet ready to practice Tree Grow?

One afternoon, as Rapunzel arranged flowers for a heart-tonic, Melinda approached and asked how it was going with Tree Grow. The girl replied, "Oh, I feel the tree. I feel its roots," as she believed was expected of her—but it was not a truthful reply, and the shame of the lie cut her. She felt her face grow hot with blushing.

Melinda heard the discomfort in Rapunzel's voice, and was concerned. But Rapunzel seemed well. She applied herself to her studies, memorizing ways to thin congestion, reduce a fever, shorten flu and comfort a cold. The month before, she had studied setting broken bones with poultices that reduce swelling and pain while nourishing the bone for quicker healing. And Rapunzel worked hard in the garden, deepening her understanding of the tastes, properties and uses of the plants.

Now a strange thing happened. Rapunzel became aware that people from the village would often knock and enter Melinda's home through a back door in the earliest hours of morning. She wondered how was it possible that she had not noticed them before? They arrived and departed while all was dark. But still. She had lived there so many years, and she hadn't seen them? Perhaps she had not been ready to see them.

When she asked Melinda about it, the old woman seemed relieved. She said that the village people came for advice and healing, for while many suspected she might be a witch, they recognized that she often brought healing when the priests and doctors could not.

Rapunzel now assisted Melinda, hands-on, in the small clinic. She met villagers, farmers and smithies, and their wives and children, while tending their ailments, and occasionally even assisting in childbirth. Soon, word of the lovely girl who lived with Melinda and tended the sick was carried to the outside world.

When Rapunzel turned fifteen, a sad thing occurred. A farmer and his wife arrived at the back door late at night. The woman was heavy with child and exhausted by labor that would not proceed, and the exertions of the journey in a cart, drawn by a slow, aged horse, had tired her still more. The farmer watched anxiously as Melinda and Rapunzel tried to save the lives of the mother and child, using potions and salves of the madder root, but it was too late. The child had suffocated deep in the birthing channel, and for the mother, too, nothing could be done. Melinda gave her a strong dose of the longflower plant to dull her pain and to send her off more swiftly.

When the man broke down, Melinda sat with him many hours. Rapunzel stood by, head bowed. The man's silent flow of tears amazed her. She wished, suddenly, powerfully, that she might be loved one day so dearly. And yet, it was unimaginable—marriage to a farmer, pregnancy, babies, living and working at the side of a common village man. Without Melinda and her knowledge, what kind of life would that be?

Melinda and Rapunzel cleaned and wrapped the bodies for the journey home. Melinda brought the farmer a flask of herbal liquor. The farmer hesitated a moment before leaving. His eyes went from the old to the young woman. "Thank you," he said to both, as if emptying his soul into the words, and then he climbed onto the cart and was gone.

There were other hard times: a young man who died of a spider bite;

none of the tried-and-true salves and poultices could halt the death of the flesh. And lung disease sometimes took down the elderly with such speed that nothing would stop it. Usually, though, they could help and restore their patients, so that Rapunzel looked forward to her lessons in healing.

One day, a man approached a far corner of the property. He rode a fine horse and was richly dressed. He peered over the stonework wall into the garden, looking for Rapunzel. When he saw the girl, now sixteen years old, working among the herbs and surrounded by a pretty cloud of moths and bees, he knew that he had found her. He called, "Young lady! Over here!"

Slowly, she walked to the wall and beheld the elegant man. He was young, sturdy, and handsome. Without warning, she felt her flower open and her river begin to flow. She blushed crimson. The warm sensation in her belly filled her mind, and she found that she could not speak.

Seeing her mortification, the man wished her good day and rode on. He did not mind that she was short of words. He had heard that she was beautiful, but to his eyes she was more: she looked healthy and quite fertile, able to bear many sons. It was said that she was learned in the healing arts, and such women were valuable. He intended to return.

From another part of the garden, Melinda, observing the strange meeting, saw the girl blush red and then fall to her knees as the man rode away. Sensing that the meeting was a portent of changes to come, Melinda sat between the lavender and roses and prayed. As she focused on her inner sight, she was at first appalled. Surely, she thought, the girl must know that this man could not be for her! But then, she listened to where she felt the tree grow, and as the sound of water-flow spread out gently through her body, and a golden glow of knowing calmed her mind, her thoughts became still and clear. *Whatever happens will be right*, she perceived with confidence. All is as it should be. Now is the *Time of Choice*.

In the weeks that followed, Melinda perceived that the girl was restless and unhappy. Still, Rapunzel was devoted to her study. She reviewed how to treat an acute rash, to soothe a burn, and she learned still more about salves that pull the poison out of a spider bite. She then made a deep study into plants that chase away the ghosts of fear that plague those with a weak nervous system, and how to improve the sleep of the insomniac. She reviewed the birth herbs again, those to tone contractions, relax the mother's mind, reduce pain, prevent rapid bleeding, and to use as a wash after birth to prevent infection. Then she reviewed the milk-herbs that reduce breast swelling, improve milk flow, and that support milk making, and also the herbs to calm a baby's digestion or treat a baby's cold, herbs that are passed to the baby through the mother's milk.

But no amount of study could entirely distract Rapunzel from her inward pain and quandary, as was apparent by the sadness in her eyes, the stoop of her shoulders, and the shallow tightness of her breath. And so, Melinda spoke to her one night at dinner.

"Rapunzel, you are not yourself. What is the reason?"

The girl only needed this question to let the words rush out: "Dear Melinda, I am confused! When I was a child, I wanted nothing more than the life of a wealthy Noblewoman. I know now that the life of a healer is worthier, and that the true love of a farmer has more value than all the riches a King might offer—but I fear I cannot have any man at all. For I have touched myself. The Old Songs have made me impure! And my punishment? I cannot keep my thoughts straight or my tongue clear when I talk to a man I might like. What shall I do?"

Melinda said, "You must practice Tree Grow. You will then be calmer in the presence of the man you like. Your mind will retain a quiet manner. Your thoughts and words will be clear. You will see.

"But Rapunzel, as for the man who met you by the wall, consider this: he may be of noble blood, but his sense of what befits a woman is low. He would expect you, Rapunzel, to bear one child after another. Your births would be full of pain because you could not, by law, avail yourself of the birthing herbs. Your milk would be scanty, so you would use animal milk to feed your nervous, colicky babies, whose distraught and cranky ways will run you down. This is not the life of dreams or the answers to prayers! You should know it!"

"Ah, Melinda! How can I know it? I know nothing of the world, only of the dreams I had before I came to live with you, and of the stories I heard long ago about beautiful women who become the wives of Noblemen."

"You can know it. If you do Tree Grow, you hear inside what is true, and you know what is right for you."

"Oh, I am so unhappy!" The girl sobbed, covering her face with her hands.

"There, there..." Melinda put her arms around the girl. And then, like motherly beings everywhere, she began to think of ways to cheer the girl. "Even if you cannot have the life of your dreams, you can learn how to make yourself still more beautiful. I can show you a salve to clear your skin of that bit of acne, a potion to clear your eyes when you are tired, and a tincture to make your hair grow faster and thicker and with even more luster."

"Oh, can you, would you?"

"Certainly. We can start tomorrow. But for now, Rapunzel, you must try, truly try, to sing Tree Grow. Feel the tree grow. The roots in your hips. The trunk as your spine."

Mayana asked, "Why is the Tree Grow song so important?"

Grandmother answered, "Tree Grow teaches the mind to be rooted in the real. Each living thing must take root in what is real and then take nourishment from it." And without explaining further, Grandmother went on with the story.

Though a season had passed, the Nobleman did not forget about Rapunzel. He wanted that girl—her knowledge, her service. He rode once again to Melinda's gardens, climbed the wall and sat at its top.

Rapunzel had practiced Tree Grow every day throughout the season. She had tried her best to pretend that she was a tree and to listen inside herself and to feel the water flow, to feel it calmly circle through her body. But images of the man kept appearing to her mind to distract her. She often tended the garden or harvested the plants that grew near the spot where they met. Singing the Grandmother Song, she would hope that, should he be hidden on the other side of the wall, he would hear her voice and respond.

That day, she suddenly saw him, sitting atop the wall. He laughed and called out, "Young Beauty, come close! What is your name? And why is such a Beauty laboring in a lowly garden, and not sitting at the side of a prince?"

Rapunzel caught her breath. She felt her abdomen grow warm and her flower open. But she was not embarrassed. She walked close and looked up at the man. "My name, Sir, is Rapunzel. I am a girl of the village, come to serve and learn from Mistress Melinda the nature of illness and medicine. It is a good life, and I am honored for it."

Surprised by her boldness, she hesitated. Some inner voice, some sense of rightness, was speaking through her. It was as if the man, and the puzzle that he posed, caused her to speak her wisest words, trusting in their strength and protection.

"Rapunzel. I see," said the man. "A strange name. I am called Gregory. Now then, Rapunzel, would you like to see my fief? I, too, have a large and wondrous garden. We, too, can grow the medical plants. You could tend them, if you would like. Or perhaps you would prefer to be my wife?"

Rapunzel trembled, shaken by his words. *Did he mean what he said?* "Sir. I am bonded by my honor to this service."

"Oh, that is a shame. Yes, of course you must fulfill your pledge to your Mistress. Then again, surely your Mistress would not miss you just one afternoon? I could show you my village, my grounds, gardens, and manor? You would return here much the wiser, knowing more about the world and about the life you have refused."

She felt her will crumble: I am being offered another life? Is he giving me a choice?

She said, "One afternoon? That might be done, I suppose."

"I am glad to hear it! I will return with a second horse. Wait for me here in two weeks' time."

Gregory jumped off the wall and, with a bounce in his step, returned to his horse. Waving farewell and whistling sweet melodies, he departed.

A tear spilled down the girl's cheek. She so wanted to see his lovely gardens and manor full of servants and elegant folk. But, however imperfectly she had been doing Tree Grow, it had none-the-less already begun to root her in the real. She knew that what he offered was not as real or as valuable as what she had right there with Melinda. Yet, a part of her wanted to ignore what she knew to be real, and, for a little while at least, to believe her childhood prayers were being answered.

Melinda had observed the meeting from the house. As they sat down for supper, she asked Rapunzel about it and about what they had spoken.

"He wants to show me his fief. And—I want to see it! Oh, Melinda, I want to see what I am leaving behind by staying on the path that you and mother chose for me."

"Rapunzel, you must know that once this man has you in his land, and under his laws, he is unlikely to let you go. You would be his servant, Rapunzel, not his wife."

"But, Melinda, I am strong. I do not believe that he would force me. And if he does, I will make him bring me back. I can do it. I know it."

Melinda thoughtfully studied the girl. "Child, before you decide, you must do one last thing: you must go up to the top of the tower for a while to finish your studies. It is not hard to live there, it is pleasant, in fact, though the sound of the wind can be bothersome."

Rapunzel felt anger crawl up her spine. She could not believe what she was hearing! Melinda judges this man without ever having spoken to him! And now, I am supposed to go up and live in the tower!

"Melinda," she said, her voice trembling, "you punish me for something I would never do! Do you know me so little? Do you think that I would lose my way, should I step outside your walls?"

Melinda's eyes grew calm as she contemplated the girl. She sighed heavily and said, "I am not punishing you, Rapunzel, but giving you a chance. To live in the tower is like living in a song. During the night, look to the stars. During the day, look to the lands. Cultivate quiet study. Deepen your skills. When you have done these things, you will take the path destined to be yours. For, Rapunzel," she paused, and met the girl's eyes meaningfully, "our paths are drawn by how firmly we are rooted in the real. Someday, you will understand this. Until then, know that whatever you choose to do, and whatever happens, you are always in my thoughts and heart. Many paths lead to the fulfillment of destiny. Some are harder, filled with suffering. A mother would always choose the path of least pain for her child, but the child must travel her own path in the end. And so you will see. The choice will be yours."

Rapunzel was comforted by Melinda's quiet manner, so that when her mentor looked in the direction of the arched door, the girl's eyes followed. Suddenly curious, she went to the door and peered inside. In all the years she had lived with Melinda, some invisible force or some fear of the unknown had held her back from looking inside this archway. In the darkness, she could just make out wide steps, chiseled in stone, spiraling up the tower, disappearing into darkness. She turned back to Melinda, expecting to be given a candle, but Melinda just smiled and urged her on with gentle motions of her hand, so the girl bowed her head and entered. With her hands feeling their way along the wall, and her feet searching for the next sure step, she began the climb.

As if the darkness was not enough to bear, she soon found herself surrounded by a low, wuthering tone that grew louder as she ascended. It was the sound of the wind, entering through the upper tower windows, reverberating down the round channel with a hollow humming tone, much like a large flute. At first, she felt the vibrations in her skin, then in her bones, and her skull. With each step, the vibrations were stronger until all her muscles and even her blood seemed alive with sound and vibration. When she stepped out into the chamber that lay close to the top of the tower, the resonance stopped. Startled, she wondered if she was the same person and if this was the same world as before. The sound

seemed to have wiped her mind clean. She felt fresh and new, like a child just awakened from sleep.

The chamber was a surprise: much larger than she'd thought, and comfortable with a small bed and feather blanket, a fireplace and crackling fire, and a flickering candle on a table. She walked to a window and looked out, but was taken aback by the closeness of the stars. She'd never seen so many before! Her head spun, and for a moment, fear overcame her—but, just as quickly, she felt safe again. She settled into bed. Listening to the soft rush of the night wind, she fell into a restful sleep.

The next morning, she awoke eager to discover her new world. She found a cupboard laden with bread, cheese, dried fruit, seeds and nuts, long-lasting root vegetables, eggs and dried meat that were perfectly edible, and pots and pans for cooking. Flasks of spring water and vats of dried grains were enough to last her several weeks. From a stack of wood near the hearth, she stoked the fire. Now her interest was drawn to a wide wooden shelf upon which she found a strange collection of books. Some were old, inscribed on sheets of treated leather that were tough enough to last for centuries. She found books on astronomy, astrology, mathematics, medicine, architecture and history. Rapunzel marveled: Whoever knew there was so much you could learn? She removed one book, opened it, saw pictures of stars in the night sky, and read their names. Suddenly she knew: this was going to be fun. She could lean out the windows and find the same stars in the sky that were here in the book.

In a cupboard she discovered familiar tools: scales and weights, flasks of various sizes, jars of herbs, stones, resins, bones and oils. She could practice making salves, tinctures and extracts.

Now a strange book caught her eye. Rather than made of bound sheets of leather, it was made of single sheets that were stacked and held together in a bundle with straps of wool. The book smelled curiously, as with traces of essential oils and perfumes. She untied the straps, lay back the cover and read the title: "The Old Songs and their Meanings." She lay back the next leather sheet, and the next. Here was Flower and Cup, and here was the Grandmother Song: detailed descriptions, instructions, and lengthy explanations. There were many authors, for the pages were written in different scripts and often signed by a different name, though the same author sometimes signed several pages. She gradually understood: this book was a collection of the thoughts and experiences of the mentors and students who had lived and worked in this tower. Some pages were written on old, browned leather, with letters so odd and words so unusual that she could not decipher them. Other pages were easy to understand—they must have been written more recently.

Rapunzel found an illustration of Tree Grow, deemed the most important song of all by one of the ancient mentors. She read how the force of the river moves along channels in the body, nourishing the organs and leading to long life that is free from disease. The song also leads to a perfect inward quietude. On one of the pages, she found the words, "Silence, Silence, Stillness, Gentle Living Stillness, Indescribable Gentle Silence." She let the words wash over her, trying to imagine the experience of the woman who had written them.

When Rapunzel came to the *Tower Song*, she stopped. *Wasn't she living the Tower Song now?* She read: "The tower represents the spine, it is the ladder between the 'above' and the 'below.' Below the tower, everyday life unfolds. At the top of the tower, powers of the mind and spirit flow free." The author went on to describe exercises that keep the spine supple. She talked about energy spots up and down the spine, and about how, in the chamber at the top of the spine—just as at the top of the tower—we can develop the strength of sight and of thought. And again, Rapunzel found pages of detailed descriptions along with illustrations, one of which caught her eye: *Ascent of Sound*. She read, "Just as the stairwell of the tower creates a dense vibration that rings in the bones, so, too, when the life force ascends the tower of the spine, we are filled with an internal vibration. That is how one knows that the inner tower is active." She turned over a few more pages and found an entry called the *Mirror Song*. She read about calm water, about the distortion of the mind, and about "*She in the Mirror*," but found it to be most confusing. *I must not be ready for this song*, she thought, and closed the book with a sense of wonder.

Later that day, Rapunzel sat by a westerly window and thought about the world. She watched all the birds: each kind flying at its own height, some above the clouds, some just above the trees. She watched the clouds: the thin lacy mists moving quickly high in the sky, and the low billowing rain clouds, hugging the hills. She walked from window to window, looking from one distant village or settlement to the next—she could just make out the color of the thatch rooftops, and she saw fields all around, golden, ready for harvest. *To feed all the people is a tremendous task, and a farmer is the most important person of all,* though they lead one of the lowliest lives. Large manors stood apart from the villages, up upon hills and surrounded by green pastures. These were the homes of the noble people. She could imagine servants cleaning and cooking, and stablemen tending the horses. The noble people were like the birds that flew at the top of the sky, she thought, high as circling hawks. *But were they therefore better than the birds of the fields?*

The next day, Rapunzel got to work deepening her skills, as Melinda had told her to do. If she was not making a medicinal preparation, she was studying a book, and if she was not reading a book, she was practicing Tree Grow. Sometimes, she attempted the practice called The Tower, guiding her breath up and down her body, as described on one of the pages in the book. But while she noticed a new quietness of mind, and a new kind of gentle alertness, she could not hear the buzzing sound from within that she had heard in the stairwell. *I must not be ready*, she thought, and then tried again.

Each morning and evening, Melinda would enter silently, replace the chamber pot and bring fresh water. She signaled that they were not to speak. But one day she murmured, "Tomorrow, expect a visitor."

That day, Rapunzel awoke in her usual working mood. In no time, her workspace was a mess of herbs, wax, oils, flasks, pans, instruments and books, as she had decided to make a pessarie, a salve and a dye, each from the madder root. She had not forgotten about her visitor, but the mess did not concern her because she was sure that Melinda would call her downstairs when the visitor arrived.

She heard steps coming up the stairwell. She stood and prepared to go down with Melinda. But a man entered the room. He was about thirty years old, had a circle of short hair around a bald skull, and he wore a long dark cloak. He was clearly a priest, Rapunzel could see that for herself, yet he seemed perfectly at ease and not in the least bothered by the chaos of herbs, simmering pots, flasks, and wax around Rapunzel. He looked at her as though he had known her a long time.

Somewhat embarrassed, she said, "Hello, Sir."

The man responded with a wide, childlike smile and sat himself down on a chair. After examining the items on the floor and table, he looked her straight in the eye and said, "This appears to be the first attempt of a hard-working student to mix medicine and magic and clean her teeth, all at the same time." Deep and friendly laughter followed his remark. Rapunzel's tension eased, and she too had to laugh. Pointing at a decoction, the man said, "If you add honey right at the end, when the potion is cool, it will be more potent in healing."

Rapunzel countered, "But the book says..."

"The book," he interrupted, "is only a collection of ideas. It is never as alive or able to learn and grow as you are right now. Remember that."

Rapunzel reached for the glass of honey and, without giving it a second thought, said, "For healing nice and fast, add the honey last."

Then the priest noticed a pot of red madder root dye and said, a serious tone in his voice, "The plant has another purpose, one not permitted. Do you know it?"

"Yes, Sir: one cup of madder root tea each day before and during moon-time and the blood will flow." She stopped and caught her breath, amazed at how easily and frankly she had spoken to this priest about forbidden things. "Melinda says that we can safely drink mild infusions of madder leaf or root tea to move the blood. She says that if a woman is not old enough, strong enough, or healthy enough to carry a child, the madder tea will release the child from the womb. But if the mother and child are strong, the child will stay. Also, at the time of birth, the same infusions move the birth forward and prevent the child from stalling in the womb. Yes, red madder prevents the deaths of mothers and children during childbirth. It is the great protector plant, and so we use it to dye our most precious clothing. Melinda tells me that such lore is forbidden, but that we may use it secretly if we do not speak about it to the priests or to our husbands."

Melinda appeared from the stairwell. She gazed approvingly at her student as she introduced the man to her as Jonathan. "Go on, Rapunzel, tell us more."

Rapunzel spoke softly: "The lore of Old Ways says that the red color of the madder root is sacred because it represents women's blood. The blood of life. But the New Way says that the red color is the blood shed by the One on the Cross—and so the priests forbid us from using red madder root to protect the lives of mothers and children."

For the remaining hours of the day, the three sat together, looking through books and discussing their contents. Once, Melinda turned to Rapunzel to explain that although Jonathan was a priest, he was also, like many priests, in the business of copying books. She had offered their most secret book to Jonathan to copy, the Book of Old Songs and their Meanings because she was afraid that, should something happen to her or to the tower, a fire perhaps, or a raid, the book and its knowledge would be lost.

Jonathan had a sad, tired expression in his eyes as he explained to Rapunzel that he was indeed copying many old books and storing them in a secret place. "If the priesthood ever learns what I am doing, my life would be done. Yet, you can be assured, for I am not alone. Many treasure the old healing lore and wish to keep it safe." Then Melinda explained to Rapunzel that because of the risk, only very few priests were actively engaged in preserving the Old Books at any one time.

Rapunzel was fascinated by the story of the priests who copy secret books. She was also impressed by what Jonathan said about the books as he inspected them. *Such a knowledgeable man,* she thought. *He even knows the secret lore.*

In particular, one thing that he said stayed in her mind, and she heard his voice repeat it again and again: "Especially if you are young, be careful not to do things too routinely, or to spend too much time with books. Your mind can get so used to it that it can lose the active spirit.

When you lose that spirit, your thinking becomes lazy and you yourself become like an old book, a collection of motionless ideas and stories. To keep your youthful spirit alive, concentrate on whatever you are doing, do it completely, and never be lazy, especially when approaching the new and unknown."

She was not lazy, but she had already observed how long reading would sometimes keep her from doing the different exercises and singing the Old Songs. What Jonathan said made good sense, and she was grateful for his advice. He also told her that he would soon return, and that he would bring tools and ink to begin copying right there in the tower.

Days passed, but he did not return. She worried about him. Sometimes, as she rubbed the high-potency tincture into her hair, she thought back to the days when she was sure that her beauty was going to fetch her a Nobleman and an easy life, a life without old books and their protectors. She smiled at that notion now, a child's fantasy.

One morning very early, during the hours when Melinda was with her patients, Rapunzel looked down from the tower and saw Gregory sitting at the wall where they had arranged to meet. He had come there often, hoping to see her, but she had been too engaged in her studies to notice. Without stopping to consider, she called down to him, "Gregory, look up! I am here in the tower!"

Following the sound of her voice, he recognized her tiny form in a window. "Rapunzel, what has happened? Are you locked up in the tower to protect you from me?"

"Yes. No! I am not locked up, but I will not go down. And it is to protect me from me, not from you. Oh, it's complicated. And it's no use that you come here. Go away!"

"I will not go! I must see you!"

Rapunzel went on: "Oh, please, go away! I do not have any time to see you now. And I do not want to visit your fief. I am content with the gardens here. Oh, please, leave me be!"

"But Rapunzel, radiant and wise Rapunzel, how can you possibly know these things? The old woman's words have beguiled you."

"But I do know, Gregory! I know—because I know!"

"You speak foolishly! That is not like you! You must see my beautiful gardens! I will climb up to your window in the middle of night and bring a long rope for you to descend upon. Give me your word that you will come with me! I will be here every day, and will bother, pine, and sing until you give me the chance that I deserve."

"Gregory," she called down to him. "Do I have your solemn and sacred vow that you will allow me to return as soon as I choose?"

"Oh, please, you insult me. I would not be a gentleman if I should force a lady. Of course you can do as you will. Always."

"Do you swear it?"

"By my mother."

"Oh, alright then. What you suggest is possible. Melinda said that I could choose. But only a brief visit, do you hear? I will not be away for more than twelve hours!"

"Agreed! I will climb up to you tomorrow in the early morning when it is still dark, and you will return before evening, I promise you!"

He rode away on his horse, but Rapunzel sat before the fire and tried to calm her mind. "Quiet now, quiet now, I'm a river," she sang. But she could not find quietude in the Tree Grow song. *Why had she told him she would go with him like that, secretively, in the dark*? If she were exercising choice, she should go by light of day, openly telling Melinda what she was doing. But, for some reason she did not understand, she could not change her plans. She felt stuck, as if something very old and greater than herself was moving her to do this thing.

Her heart was racing now, her thoughts spinning. *What if he does not allow me to return*? If I am not strong enough to make him bring me back? Is such a thing possible, or am I imagining such horrors due to Melinda's whisperings?

Just after lunch, that same day, Melinda called Rapunzel downstairs. Two guests had arrived: her mother and her little sister, Susanne. A year had passed since the girls had last visited together. Both had visibly changed. Susanne was now twelve years old, while Rapunzel was sixteen. "You two should become acquainted again," said their mother.

Susanne was very beautiful—more beautiful even than Rapunzel had been at her age. Yet Rapunzel did not feel even a tiny pang of envy for her sister's loveliness. She understood now that beauty was not a thing that is mystically granted, undeserved, but is rather the result of her mother eating a more nourishing diet before and during pregnancy. All children should be healthy and beautiful, she thought.

Susanne approached her sister. "What amazing hair you have," she said.

"Oh, that's all the thistles and bitter herbs from the garden that I eat at mid-day. But I also use a hair potion that Melinda showed me. It strengthens the roots. I'll make you some."

The two girls smiled warmly and clasped hands. Rapunzel said, "Come up to my room. There is so much to see there." They glanced at Melinda, who motioned them to go.

They climbed the spiral stairs, adding the sound of laughter to the wuthering hum. The women in the room below heard their laughter and smiled warmly. The partnership between Lyla and Melinda had been good. Both girls were doing well. Melinda now explained the reason that she had sent for them at short notice: the young man who returned often to the wall was surely tempting Rapunzel to go away with him. "We agree that the girl must have the freedom to choose—she is of the age for it. I am imparting as much of the teaching as possible to her now, to strengthen her."

Lyla answered, "In the name of Rapunzel, thank you for all you have done. She is young, yet she is old enough to choose. Of course, I came as soon as you sent word. Also, so that you may see Susanne and give me more advice for her."

Up in the tower, Susanne looked in amazement through all the books and instruments, while Rapunzel mixed a brew of hair potion.

"I am glad to be here with you again," said Susanne. "Tell me, is it true that you no longer think of marriage as you once did, and no longer care to become a Nobleman's wife?"

"Oh, yes, I suppose that I have changed, though I do not yet know what I think about marriage. I feel pulled in different ways. There was a farmer who lost his wife in childbirth. The way he looked at her—I would like to be loved like that. But could I leave my life with Melinda to be a farmer's wife? Or would a farmer be a partner to me in the Old Ways— letting me live here with the child and bringing us companionship and food? I do not think so. A farmer needs a wife to work at his side. And then, Susanne, there is one man... He is in the Church but he respects the Old Traditions. Oh, Susanne, he is knowledgeable, and his wisdom makes me warm and comfortable. But could such a man have a wife? Or would he agree to a partnership in the Old Ways? I do not know. I believe it would be too dangerous for him to do so. And, yes, Susanne, there is one Nobleman I do see sometimes. He flatters me. But it is not as you think. I am not sure what to think of it myself. I suppose people are already talking about us! He must have spoken about me to his friends. They will want to know where he goes when he rides out to see me. He might have divulged our plan. But what is our plan?" She was talking more to herself now than to her sister. Startled by her uncertain and chaotic thoughts, she looked up at Susanne. "Truly, I do not wish to go with him. My life is here!"

Susanne was concerned for her sister, but then she saw a sly, jesting expression appear in Rapunzel's eyes. "I have an idea," Rapunzel said, "Since I cannot tell you exactly what I feel about this man, because I do not know myself, let me tell you a story—just as the people in the village would tell it."

Susanne laughed. "Make it as silly as possible, Sister."

"It begins—with a pregnant woman who craves a certain herb, and with a witch who says she can have it only on one condition: that she hand over her first-born child. The mother, terrified of evil spells, agrees, and when the child is born, she tearfully places her baby daughter, whose name is Root, into the witch's arms.

"Now, the witch hates the girl because she hates all humans—but she hates her all the more because she is beautiful. She locks the girl up in a tower so no one can see her, nor she anyone. The witch then gives her a magic potion to make her hair grow long and full, and it becomes so long, thick, and heavy that Root cannot move. Her only activity is to brush her hair from morning to night.

"All is not lost for Root because a young Nobleman hears about the beautiful girl and decides to rescue her. In the darkness of night, he stands beneath her window and entreats her to leave the tower so that he can take her away on his horse. But she calls down that she can not go—because her hair is long and heavy and she cannot move. So he says, 'Throw down your hair and I will use it to climb up to your window.' The girl does as she is told. He climbs into her room, draws his sword, hacks off her hair and then carries the girl, who is too weak to walk, down the steep, winding stairs of the tower.

"The witch is waiting for them at the bottom, with her evil wand held aloft. Luckily, on the last step the man trips and falls—and he and Root are catapulted onto the witch, who is struck down so suddenly that she has no time to cast a spell upon them. Now the man puts his sword through the witch's heart, and green blood drains from her body. The girl is rescued, and can go off and be the wife of a Nobleman!"

Susanne clapped her hands. "How gruesome and wonderful!"

"Yes, dear Sister, but it is just a story. Imagine—thinking Melinda could be a witch! But the real story and how it might unfold is still unknown, for the young man does desire me to go with him to see his home and grounds, Sister."

"Don't you want to have the life of a Noblewoman?"

"I guess, if I am honest with myself, there is a part of me that still longs for that life. But, just as honestly, I can tell you that I no longer want an easy life. There is so much to do, to learn, Susanne, to help the people, and too few who are able to do it!"

"Susanne! Rapunzel!" Their mother was calling. "Time to go! Come down now!"

As the sisters descended the winding stairs in darkness, a premonition of fear befell them: with strange certitude, they knew that their world was changing, and that they very well might not see one another again.

In the main room once more, Rapunzel regained her composure. She turned to Susanne and asked her to come again soon.

Susanne tried to speak calmly. "I will come, Sister, though my help is dearly needed at home. Until then, I wish you well."

"Before you go," Rapunzel said, softly, moving close to her sister's ear, "I must ask if you know the Grandmother Song?"

"Yes, Mother taught me, as Melinda instructed her to do," Susanne said, reassuringly. "And I know Tree Grow."

"Then all is well."

The sun shone down on the hill from directly overhead. Mayana opened her eyes. Cascading rays of light, shooting down between the leaves and the shadows, were catching as a blaze in Grandmother's hair. Mayana thought about all the seasons of change that Grandmother had seen over her long life. A feeling of sadness befell her, as she sensed how quickly her own life would pass, and how fragile all the things that gave her strength and comfort might turn out to be.

Suddenly, she saw another old woman's face, hovering just before her grandmother's familiar features. It was Melinda, she was sure. But before she could tell Grandmother what she saw, the apparition smiled at her, as if saying hello, and disappeared.

Only Grandmother's eyes now gazed at Mayana.

Did Grandmother truly know Melinda, Susanne, and Rapunzel? Did they live inside her? Mayana recalled Grandmother saying that when these stories were told to her as a girl, they became like her own memories.

Mayana smiled shyly at her mentor, realizing and accepting that she herself might soon become the receptacle of these lives and memories. For this was her *Time of Choice*, and she understood with new clarity, just now, that she was choosing to receive the teachings.

Into the sacred stillness of their shared, wordless understanding, Mayana asked, "How does the story go on? What happens to Rapunzel, Melinda, and Susanne?"

"As you wish, Mayana. I will tell you. Close your eyes."

Remember, it is the *Time of Choice*. Rapunzel has chosen to meet Gregory in the darkness of night. Melinda does not stop her, but from a window high up in the tower she watches as they ride away. Gregory, as Melinda predicted, will indeed force Rapunzel to stay at his fief, calling upon a law that is specifically designed to limit the rights of the women who follow the Old Ways. His plan for her is to replicate the beauty of Melinda's garden at his own estate. He also wants her to teach his farmers all that she knows about agriculture, and his doctors all that she knows about healing. He visits Rapunzel at night, trying for a son, but she takes the red madder and other herbs to move her blood each month, and so she does not carry his seed.

Many years pass with Rapunzel remaining captive in his fief. She cannot show Gregory's farmers and doctors as much as she might have, had she completed her studies with Melinda, but she devotes her talents to the tasks at hand and improves the lives of his people. She is known as a healer and the people from all around seek her service. Her reputation spreads as fewer women die in childbirth. The babies, flourishing on their healthy mother's milk, grow to be strong and attractive.

"Her sister, Susanne, will live long with Melinda and learn the crafts thoroughly. She will carry on Melinda's line and become a great mentor.

Like Rapunzel, she will do much to spread the wisdom of the Old Ways back among the people.

"But Mayana, understand: as the people's lives improve and more boys grow into strong men, able to wield weapons, more armies are sent off to war. A new generation is enamored with battle. And these men are jealous of the women's knowledge. And so begin the burnings of the women they call witches, across all the lands and for hundreds of years."

Mayana bolted upright and stood. As Grandmother had spoken of the burnings, she'd seen as a vision many thousands of women, girls, boys, and some men, too, like Jonathan, roped above piles of wood and set ablaze by men standing by with stern faces, terrified of losing their power.

Mayana fell to the ground and wept. The earth tumbled and spun as she sank into pain and darkness. It was her dream again, the screaming children, the endless suffering she could not stop or endure.

When the light finally found her, it was just a pinpoint, a tiny spark, far away. As it grew larger, she found herself in a long line of women. Just behind her was Grandmother. Far ahead she could see Susanne, standing tall, her fair hair whipping about her shoulders. Susanne was grieving for her sister.

Mayana pushed herself onto her feet. With her head thrown back and her fists clenched tight, she summoned all the power of her grief and danced, slowly at first and then faster, a stamping of pain in the grass. Grandmother closed her eyes and listened to the drumming story, to the unrelenting cycles of becoming and ceasing. Her head fell forward and she sank into herself again, a frail old woman once more.

Mayana's dance grew softer and slow. Finally, she sat on the stone, her shoulders shivering, her jaw trembling, but her gaze gentle, and direct. "It is as you said, Grandmother. The sadness. The responsibility. How can I bear it? The farther ahead I stretch my sight, the more sorrow I see."

Grandmother raised her eyes and looked intently at Mayana. She said, "Sadness is also a teacher. It can show us who we are. Those who are rooted in the real will understand much sorrow. As for strength, Mayana, you *do* have strength to bear it—even to bear the teachings of your own broken heart.

"But the day moves on. The sun has passed overhead and soon seeks the western mountains. I must teach you more about The Tower. Are you ready to receive this teaching?"

Mayana, her cheeks still glistening with tears, gathered her focus and straightened her spine. She said, solemnly, "Grandmother. Please begin."

Grandmother spoke: "Like Tree Grow, The Tower is practiced to nourish all the inner parts of the body, and especially to heal the spine. But The Tower has another meaning. It is about habits of thought and feeling that can choke the life force. Like vines that climb and strangle a tree, vines and ivy can darken the walls of a tower as they cling to it year after year.

"There is a story told about this, Mayana, about a girl who sleeps for a hundred years in a tower that is surrounded by a thorny hedge. The girl cannot wake up. She is in the tower, and she should be learning the lessons of The Tower, but she cannot learn them because her mind is strangled by thoughts and emotions that are mere habits, and not truly alive and responsive. She is asleep to her own life! In the story, the thorns are eventually cut down. The tower is released from their grip, and the girl awakens."

Mayana was grateful for what she recognized as an important teaching. She memorized it, breathed it into her mind and body, closed her eyes and felt her way inside. At first, she was aware of the calm feeling of quiet that comes with Tree Grow. Then she saw and felt her spine as a tower. The two are similar, she thought, but different as well. Tree Grow is quieter, gentler, and The Tower is more focused.

Grandmother saw that Mayana was working through the teachings and was glad. She had not yet told Mayana, but she had a reason to press forward. She said, "Mayana, there is something I would like to ask you."

"Grandmother?"

"Tell me, why were you frightened yesterday? You have been alone in the forest many times before."

Mayana smiled at the simplicity of the question—she knew: the simplest questions often lead to the greatest insights. She said, "I don't know. I was walking through Cattail Valley, digging out young stalks at the bank of the creek, when I felt the hills loom up on the east side. I breathed deeply to send the fear out of my body, but I could not be rid of it. I felt that someone is watching me. Fear overcame me again and again, always stronger, until I began to run, as fast as I could, to your hut. And yet, the fear still followed, a shadow-ghost of danger. I thought to myself that this would be how people feel who are chased by a wolf or a bear. And so I put the wolf into the story that I told Carmona."

Grandmother said, "It is clear to me now. You have told me that you have sung the Grandmother Song, but you have not practiced it fully, have not known the dance of the hands. But you have both sung and practiced Tree Grow—you have befriended silence, have felt the force that circles throughout your body, and that is good. But, like Rapunzel, you need both songs for balance, as you need both feet to walk upright. You, Mayana, have not yet met the wolf in your body. So it came to you, seemingly from outside, as a presence in the forest. Your unknown wolf became your unnamed fear."

Mayana felt faint for a moment as a flood of insight nearly overwhelmed her. "Grandmother, I see," she said, trembling, opening her eyes wide. "I believe I know what you are saying. But how is it possible?"

Gently and slowly her mentor replied, "It is possible because we are very much older than our body-age. And when your own body-wolf does not protect you, you are not safe from your ancient memories. They will come. Sometimes they feel like sadness, or anger, or fear. But if you befriend your body-wolf, these memories will not have such power over you. Mayana, you must practice the Grandmother Song, but do not neglect Tree Grow."

"Yes. Thank you, Grandmother. I see it now."

A warm breeze moved through and between the Story Tree's leaves—it was the tree's own voice, singing the *Song of Sharing*.

Great joy, one mind meets another...
Great joy, one heart knows another...

It was afternoon. The sun's heat began to break. A breeze teased their hair and cooled their skin. Mayana looked up into the tree's many branches. Some branches swayed low like the arms of a mother stooping to embrace her child. Some stretched upward, like the arms of the hunter with his bow. Mayana knew herself protected.

The next story that Grandmother tells has to do with sight. It is about a girl and her mother who learn to see clearly, themselves and each other.

Looking Past
The Looking Glass —
Deep Mirror Song

"Do you know the *Deep Mirror Song*?"

Fahrwa whined and tapped his tail.

Mayana shook her head, no. "What is it about?"

Grandmother's eyes grew playful.

"It is about how we see. Most people believe that we see with our eyes, but the eyes do not see fully."

Mayana thought about Grandmother's words. She, too, believed that she saw with her eyes. *Was she wrong?*

Grandmother sang:

I see me,

I see you,

In the mirror.

Through the mirror

I see only You—

I flow to You

Like a river—

You look through

And see all of us.

Mayana frowned. She said, "I have not heard this song. What is so special about this mirror, and who is it that looks through the mirror and sees all of us?"

Grandmother chuckled. "It is not a riddle, Mayana. Think! When you see a stone that lies in water, you do not see the stone fully. You must first take the stone out of the water to know its color and form. And just so, we also see the world through a kind of distortion, a distortion of the mind. We do not see true at all.

"But, Mayana, if you make your mind as quiet as the surface of a pond that reflects your face perfectly back to you—then you can see through the surface of things to the depths. You can see the stone's form. You can see the world fully. But we must practice a long time to quiet the mind, and to see it."

Mayana shifted uncomfortably.

Grandmother went on, "But the song speaks to something else as well. It says that when the mind is fully quiet, we see into the world of the Great Mother of Life. She is both a vast ocean and a perfectly reflective pool. When she looks into herself, she finds all things: you, and me, and all of us."

Grandmother laughed at Mayana's worried expression. "Practice the Deep Mirror song. You will find the mystery of who you are—and only you can find it."

Mayana closed her eyes and sat as still as she could. She imagined the surface of a pond, all the waves and ripples becoming still. A scowl settled on her face from the effort. Finally, she opened her eyes and said, frustration in her voice, "It is not easy to find the practice in your words, Grandmother."

The old woman laughed. "I will tell you a story to help you understand. It is about a girl and a mirror. But, like all tales, it only points at the thing behind the words; your mind may get caught in the distracting glass of the story, rather than seeing what is deep within it. Close your eyes. Listen."

Now Grandmother did not laugh and her eyes were not playful. She spoke seriously, telling a tale that is familiar to us all as the story of Snow White.

In the age that follows Rapunzel's time, the daughters of the Noble class fulfill an important role and so they must learn a great many things. Indeed, they learn far more than their brothers, who learn to wield weapons and to master the logic of battle, but rarely manage even the basics of reading or math. As men, they visit one another's manors, go out hunting together on horseback, gather their serfs into battle to raid and to steal, and, when commanded by the King, they gladly leave their fiefdoms for years at a time, off in the business of war.

The Noblewomen manage their husbands' fiefs. They attend to the slaves, the serfs, and the animals. They sit as judges at local courts. They arrange that goods are purchased and transported into the fiefdom. To do these many things, the girls study law, accounting, medicine, agriculture, and husbandry. But more than all this: they learn to act fairly and with compassion—or else risk losing the respect of the people, and losing their control over the fiefdom.

Times are often hard, Mayana. Drought and famine frequent the lands. Hunger comes and goes with the seasons. In summer, before the first planting has ripened, the fief-folk stretch their flour with ground-up herbs that they find in the meadows. Before the autumn harvest, they stretch their remaining gruel with the ground-up bark of trees. But while struggling with fatigue and weakness, they look forward to the yearly festivals and bountiful feasts that mark the end of the hunger seasons, festivals that are arranged for and overseen by Noblewomen who understand how to lead the fief-folk through the yearly cycles of work, toil, hunger and celebration.

In one such fief lived a Noblewoman named Felicia. Her husband had been away on the business of war for so many years that Felicia no longer counted on his return. Felicia lived with her two daughters: Clare, the younger, and Prudence, the older. The servants called Prudence "Snow White," for she was pale of skin and fond of her delicate appearance.

The name Felicia means happiness. It was given by her mother, in the hope that she would find joy in her life of duty. And Felicia did find satisfaction in managing the fief and in raising her daughters. Similarly, she named her oldest daughter Prudence, in the hope that it would give her the level-headedness needed to be a Nobleman's wife.

Prudence's education began at four when she was obliged to assist in the gardens. Over the next ten years, until marriageable at fourteen, she should learn the basics of farming and husbandry, and study arithmetic, accounting, history and law. Each of these skills would be needed for her future role.

Prudence was a pretty girl. The nutritional knowledge that Melinda had passed on through Rapunzel and Susanne was now widely known and used, also by the Noblewomen. Therefore, people in general were healthier. The women had more children. More boys could grow into strong, healthy men to tend the fields and grow more food, but also more men could be sent off to war.

Crafts and trades flourished. Small businesses thrived through a new kind of market that sold articles of usefulness and luxury to the noble families. One of these crafts was a new method to make mirrors. To look at oneself in one of these new, silver-backed mirrors was to see oneself perfectly reflected. Felicia bought several of the new mirrors to hang in her manor. She liked the way they lit up the rooms with light reflected from candles and windows, and she liked that she could briefly glance at a mirror and check if her hair was right. But the light-catchers had a different effect on Prudence. The girl could now often be found standing before a mirror and staring at her image in rapture, as if cast beneath a spell. To break the mirror-spell, Felicia would first firmly call Prudence's name. Then she'd shake her gently by the shoulder. Finally, with her hands on her daughter's cheek and chin, she'd forcefully turned her daughter's gaze away from the mirror.

Prudence's head would tremble and her eyes appear startled as she came out of the trance and saw her mother's concerned expression. Felicia would now tell Prudence that her tutors were complaining, for she was often absent from class. But sadly, though Prudence returned to class the very next morning, by mid-day she would again be found standing mesmerized before one of the mirrors.

"Daughter, there is something I must tell you," Felicia said one morning, after turning the girl's face to her own and waiting for the life to return to Prudence's startled eyes.

"When I was young, we did not have such mirrors. Our mirrors were not smooth, so the image was not clear. But long ago, people had no mirrors at all. They had to view their reflections in water. They would sit by a pond and wait a long time for a perfect moment of stillness, without ripples or waves. When they finally saw themselves, or so say the old tales, they were so calm in their minds that they could see right through their image to who they really were. Do you understand? *See who you really are.* There were songs about it once. Supposedly, the songs instructed young women in how to see—without getting caught in the trap of sight. But today, these mirrors hang in all the manors! I have received letters from across the land. Everywhere it is the same. Mothers complain that their daughters are losing their souls in the mirrors. Just like you, they stare at themselves for hours, trying their hair this way and that, fretting about their figures and dresses. Just like you, they neglect their studies and are oblivious to everything that they must learn to become respected and capable Noblewomen."

As Felicia spoke, a strange thing happened. Snow White heard her mother's words, but she did not understand their meaning, not even a tiny part of it. She thought: "My mother is jealous because she is not as young and beautiful as I am. That is why she does not like me to look in mirrors." But Prudence replied, hoping to appease her mother without revealing her thoughts, "Yes, Mother. I will be careful not to lose my soul in the mirror."

Weeks passed, and the girl's teachers continued to complain. Felicia did not know what to do. Nothing she said seemed to make any difference. Finally, she ordered the servants to remove the mirrors from the walls and to lock them all up in her chamber.

That morning, when Prudence emerged from her room and was met by empty walls, her anger knew no bounds. *I hate my mother!* she said to herself. *And she clearly despises me!* She is insane—insanely jealous! She cannot bear how pretty I am! She probably stands in front of a mirror herself when she thinks no one is looking, comparing her wilting skin to my fresh beauty!

Prudence stormed through the manor. She found Felicia in the library, quietly reading as she often did in books on law, to be prepared that day to act as judge at court. The girl pressed her fists onto her waist and screamed: "I want the mirrors back on the walls, now!"

Her mother's eyes widened with alarm, but after taking a moment to regain her calm, she explained: "You cannot understand this now, but what I have done is for your own good. Your youth is passing—a precious time for learning that will never return—while you have nothing on your mind but admiring yourself in shiny sheets of glass. Sometimes I think," her voice broke, "I think your soul is already lost! The soul of your whole generation! What will become of you? How will you fulfill your responsibilities? How will you teach your own daughters the skills and knowledge necessary to lead and manage whole fiefdoms?"

Beneath the Story Tree, Mayana opened her eyes. With wonderment in her voice, she said, "But Grandmother, Felecia spoke plainly! How is it possible that Prudence did not understand her clear words and meaning?"

Grandmother laughed and slapped her hands on her thighs. "It can be almost funny when someone speaks clearly but is not understood. It is because of mind's distortion. Listen: Can you think of a reason, Mayana, that to see ourselves in water requires patience? What if we could see ourselves easily, any time that we wished? How would that affect the minds of those who are not secure in the Old Songs, and not at all secure in the Mirror Song?"

Mayana scowled even more. "I do not care much about seeing myself in the water. Though I do like the game of seeing ourselves in the black pools of each other's eyes. Still, what if I could easily see myself? Would I really wish to look at nothing else, Grandmother?"

"If you were not grounded in the Old Songs, Mayana, you might look at nothing else. You might believe that there is nothing else of value to see. Could you free yourself of the spell that your reflection casts? For in that reflection, you might believe that you know your true value, and that you know how others see you—namely, exactly as you see yourself. And so your view of yourself, and of others, would be small.

"Others never see us as we see ourselves. They see us through the distortions of their minds. For instance, if they see themselves through the attainment of learning, or lack of it, they will see what you have learned in comparison to them. If they see and value themselves through their skills, such as farming, science, or art, they will see how well you do these things in comparison to them. If they see themselves as above or below other people, they will see you as higher or lower than themselves. If they possess the virtues of patience, compassion, and love, they will see those virtues budding in you, and appreciate your potential. But if they see themselves as being a person of vice and meanness, they will try to pull you into their vice as well. But if a whole generation of girls is convinced that how they perceive themselves in the mirror is how others perceive them as well, if they think that their appearance is in fact the measure of who they are, their minds become small, like the shallow glass into which they look. They are blind to all the myriad forms of perception and self evaluation. The Deep Mirror song says that we must look through the mirror to deepen our perception, and not at it. Now let us go on. Close your eyes. Listen:"

Prudence believed that mirrors revealed an extraordinary thing: that she was becoming a woman. Her mother saw mirrors more practically. As reflectors of light, they lit up the dark rooms of her manor. Alone a quick glance sufficed to see if her hair and dress were as they should be. More than that was a waste of time and attention.

Here is how looking at mirrors changed Prudence: The more she looked, the more she believed that the way she saw herself was the way others saw her, too, or at least, was the way that they should see her, and the less she believed that her mother had her best interest at heart. Her mother, after all, must perceive her as a young beauty. Her mother must be jealous. That must be why she spoke so badly about mirrors.

When the mirrors were locked up in Felicia's chamber, Prudence felt lost. To amend that feeling, she decided that she would be loyal to the idea of the mirrors. It would now be her duty at all times to consider what her reflection in the mirror might look like if a mirror were actually there to reflect her image. She lived with an imaginary mirror, constantly in her mind, and was determined to be vigilant about the way she looked.

When her mother found her sitting next to a pile of papers and books but staring off into space, imagining what she would look like if a mirror were hanging there, Felicia was overcome with anger. She frowned and clenched her fists. The veins in her neck bulged. She looked altogether unattractive in the eyes of the girl, who, horrified to see how little her mother cared for her appearance, lost all respect for her mother in that moment.

"How does daydreaming help you?" Felicia cried. "Surely you must know that until you are competent at math, accounting, law and agriculture, you will be unable to fulfill your duties as a Noblewoman, duties upon which the wellbeing of the fiefdom relies!"

Convinced her mother's anger was fueled by envy, Prudence retorted with vigor, "If you want me to be better at school, put the mirrors back up on the walls!"

Felicia's body shook. Tears started in her eyes. Her voice broke as she said, "If you cared half as much about your schoolwork as you care about your appearance, we wouldn't be having this fight!"

But Prudence again was not able to understand the meaning of her mother's words. She mixed them all up in her mind and thought Felicia was saying, "We're only fighting because of your beautiful appearance!"

Prudence screamed at her mother with abandon: "You're jealous! You're vengeful! That is why you have taken away the mirrors, and that's why you torture me! You can't stand that I am so much prettier than you are!"

Felicia gasped and took a step back. She understood at last that nothing she might say, no matter how reasonable, would reach her daughter's mind. She blanched, turned, and withdrew.

Prudence shook with rage. She was supposed to go down to the classroom and study with her tutors, but she locked herself in her room instead and stayed there the rest of the day, not even going down to eat. Over and over, she reviewed her mother's words and actions. It must be plain meanness. What other reason could there be? Yet, at bedtime, she snuck into Clare's room and slipped into her bed for comfort.

"Tell me a story," Clare said, slinging an arm around her big sister's waist.

"I will tell you a story," Prudence said. She was suddenly inspired.

"But it is a secret and you mustn't tell anyone!" She began:

"Once there was a King who had a beautiful daughter named Snow White, just like me. His beloved wife, the girl's real mother who loved her dearly, died when the girl was young, and after a while, he remarried. But his new wife hated the girl. She was jealous of her beauty. As the girl grew ever more beautiful, the Queen could be found standing long hours in front of a mirror in her chamber, studying her face and figure in the glass, and asking the mirror again and again, 'Am I not the most beautiful woman in all the land?'

"One day, she could not deny what the mirror told her: she was not nearly as beautiful as her stepdaughter. The Queen grew sick with envy and decided there was only one thing to do: she must have the girl killed!

"She asked her trusted servant, an old Knight who had seen many battles, to take Snow White into the forest and to stab her dead. For proof of the deed, he should bring the child's heart to her in a small wooden box."

Clare shivered with excitement. "Go on with the story," she said. "What happened?"

Prudence whispered, "The old Knight was moved to mercy by the beauty and goodness of the girl, and he let her live. He killed a wild pig, put its heart in the box instead, and fooled the evil stepmother. The girl got away. I think the story actually goes on... somehow... but I cannot remember the rest."

Soon the sisters were asleep in each other's arms.

The next day, when Prudence again did not go to class, her mother again sought her out and found her in the kitchen, where she was eating leftovers to make up for last night's missed dinner. This time, their words were so fierce that Prudence began to wonder whether the story she had told her sister were not true. Surely this woman was evil and was plotting to have her killed! She again fled to her room, where she turned her mother's words over in her mind, trying to make sense of them. But the more she thought about it, the more certain she became that she must flee! Just like Snow White in the story, she must run for her life!

That night, as everyone in the manor slept, Prudence put on a simple dress and wrap, packed a purse with victuals, hung flasks of water over her shoulders, and slipped out through a back door. She tip-toed through the garden paths, silently opened and shut the gate, and went onto the main road. Keeping to the cover of moon-shadow, she passed through the village, then passed beyond the walls, and found her way beyond the farmer's huts, hovels and fields. An occasional dog barked at her, but no one awoke to see her sneak away.

As the sky began to lighten, she followed a gully to the river and then followed animal paths crisscrossing between bushes on the bank for several miles. When she climbed out of the channel and looked out across the land, she wondered where she should go. She knew that the river headed toward the next fiefdom where someone would surely recognize her as Felicia's daughter. But if she crossed over the countryside toward the hills far in the distance, she might find an isolated settlement with simple folk who would not know her.

She started out into the field of tall grasses. Tiny-winged, low-flying insects surrounded her in a sparkling haze, and they bit and stung. She increased her stride, working up a sweat, and drank water and ate victuals without stopping. By late afternoon, she saw what looked like a small stone settlement far up on a distant hillside. She walked on for several hours more. Finally, she came to a path that led up into the hills. Soon she was walking past well-tended, terraced gardens. She could smell lovage, rosemary, thyme, and the acrid tang of rue. She fought back a surge of feeling. Her mother had taught her the herbs. "When you are grown up," she'd said, "all the skills of healing must be known to you, for you will have the care of the people." Prudence remembered a child's verse:

Blue violet, flowers and leaves
Tea with honey, the small child pleases
Soon sleeps sound with Jesus.

Sweet Vervain for blood-day pain.
Holy Vervain, the devil's bane.

When feeling weak and skin so pale,
The leaves of nettle never fail
To strengthen up your mettle.
Mary's thistle for mother's milk,
The seeds collect in summer,
Simmer in hot water,
Babe must never hunger.

Lemon Balm, the nerves to calm.
The liver heals, the great thirst stills.

With borage for melancholy,
Brings laughter and brings gladness.
The seeds soaked in wine will
Lift spirits and knit sinew,
Drunk before a fight,
Gives courage to the Knight

Peppermint for colic,
Chamomile for cramping,
Both for rest and sleeping,
Saves my babe from weeping.

Elderberry flower,
With its healing power,
Brings down baby's fever,
Speeds the course of illness
So baby's happy faster.

Purple elder berries,
Cooked and sieved to syrup,
With water hot, in a cup,
Eases heat, and softens cough.

When blood flows like a river,
Take up the Shepard's purse,
Crush with spittle on the skin
Or swallow if blood flows from within.

Red clover, red clover,
Softens tumors, we grow older,
Strengthens bones, makes us bolder,
Takes the heat from woman's shoulder.

The path ended at the gate of a high surrounding wall. She pulled on a rope that hung from the archway and a heavy bronze bell clanged. A few minutes later, the gate was unlatched and pulled open, and before her stood a wide, bearded man. His eyebrows rose thoughtfully as he took in the girl. He wore a brown, coarsely woven robe, and his drawn face was serious. It dawned on Prudence that she had arrived at a monastery—a place apart from the world where people lived, studied and worked— most of them orphaned or abandoned as babies, had lived their whole lives by the charity of the church. She was suddenly glad, relieved even, for monasteries were renowned for their hospitality. Some even had separate houses built especially for pilgrims.

The man did not say a word, but he signaled her to follow. He led her into the main building, and then to a common room warmed by a fire. Tables were set. Monks sat close to one another, stooping over bowls of steaming soup. She smelled barley, oats, carrots, cabbage, lovage, rosemary, and thyme. There was something strange about the monks. They had taken a vow of silence, but they talked excitedly with their hands and fingers, asking for more soup, bread, or for pepper. Their silent but energetic communication made Prudence laugh—she covered her mouth with her hand, so as to not offend.

Prudence was given a bowl by one of the monks and directed to a table on the other side of the room, around which sat a group of pilgrims: men and women of every age and from every walk of life, quietly eating and observing the silence expected of them at mealtime. When she finished eating, the monk who had opened the gate actually spoke to her. He asked who she was, and the room was suddenly still as everyone stopped eating to listen to her answer—for she was the youngest and prettiest pilgrim of the group.

"My name is Molly, my father is a farmer, and I am in danger of my life from my stepmother."

The monks and the pilgrims smiled, but some of them shook their heads. They could see by her hands that were not callused by the work of a farm, and by her speech that was not common, that her story was not true. But the girl was in her early teens, old enough to be married, and certainly old enough to leave home and become a pilgrim if she desired, regardless of her origins.

The monk who had spoken told her she was welcome to eat and to rest that night, and that if she chose to stay, she could labor in the house and gardens for her keep. If truth be told, the monks hoped she would stay, for they knew that a young woman alone on the road was in danger. Noblemen would not marry or even feed the girls they found traveling alone as pilgrims, and neither did marauding knights, thieves, or other such persons.

That same morning, back at the manor, Prudence's teachers again complained to Felicia. This time, the girl had not attended even one morning class. Neither had she been seen at breakfast. A servant was sent to find her in her room, but returned to say she was not there and that the bed had not been slept in. Felicia ordered the servants to find her: they should search the manor, the gardens, the grounds, and the village. As the day passed, everyone in the fief got involved in the search. They climbed down into cellars and up into attics, clambered into wells, and combed the banks of the river.

Late afternoon, Felicia could be heard mumbling to herself: "She'll turn up. She'll suddenly reappear." But with sunset, visions overcame her. She imagined Prudence kidnapped, taken into slavery, or ravaged and left to die, her broken body hidden beneath bushes or within a forest where no one would find her.

These things happen to girls and women who travel the land as pilgrims, she knew. She had not warned Prudence about such dangers; her daughter had seemed so safe within her fiefdom. *Why upset a child with worldly, fearful knowledge?* But what could have happened? Did one of her husband's enemies steal into the manor and kidnap the girl while everyone slept? Acts of vengeance were commonplace, whether between the Noblemen themselves or the knights who served them, and to steal a girl of marriageable age would be a way to settle scores. Indeed, when the men were off at war, taking their fighting and feuding far away with them, everyone felt safer, for knights knew little restraint, and no one was safe when they had drunk one mug too many.

Felicia had often considered the irony: whereas girls were skillful in many subjects, boys learned only how to fight. Yet, the priests said that men had a God-given right to rule over women. Granted, a few women of royalty were as powerful as a king, ruling in their own name, or ruling through their husbands or sons, and a few women of the Old Ways still managed to not marry and legally hold on to their property and lineage. But they were the exceptions.

Felicia had thought herself fortunate to have daughters. She had been grateful for the responsibility and the opportunity to pass down her skills and knowledge to them. It is in the way of things, after all, that a daughter will carry on her mother's legacy, which, ultimately, is the care of the people. And so it had always been.

Felicia withdrew to her chamber. Leaning against the wall stood all the mirrors of the manor. She had wanted to prevent her daughter from looking into them, but now she wanted nothing more than to see her daughter's sweet face looking out at her from within them. Her thoughts spun: Was I wrong to take the mirrors away? Am I being punished?

She crawled into bed. There she stayed, sometimes sobbing and sometimes staring aghast at the mirrors in horror, as if they were mocking her. The next day, she was awakened by sunlight shining in through her window. It reflected in the mirrors as if to torture her. She rang for the servants and begged them to darken the room—and so she would remain throughout her grieving time. She slept little, and would eat only bites of hard bread and drink only cold water. She rebuffed her servants if they urged her to eat more, and she refused to see a doctor. Days and then weeks passed, with darkness and fasting doing their work on her body and soul. Then, one morning, she sensed that her inner darkness was lifting. She got out of bed, pulled back the curtains, and stood before the mirrors. She wanted to defy their emptiness by placing her familiar shape within them. But to her surprise, in the mirrors stood a stranger.

Beneath the Story Tree, Mayana opened her eyes and said: "Didn't she see herself?"

"Yes," Grandmother said. "But her shiny brown hair was now gray. And she was thin, her muscles and warm padding wasted away. Her skin hung in waxy, sallow folds from her body and her face, and her sunken eyes, encircled by dark rings, stared back at her without expression.

"But Mayana, how she appeared in the mirror stood in stark contrast to how she actually felt, for she had grown close to herself. She did not think of herself as the decrepit, haggard, dying person that she saw in the mirror. She thought of herself as having become strong and alive in a new way. For although grief had ravished Felicia's outer person, and her body was dying, it had also dug a calm place in her heart where she could know herself. Her spirit was reborn."

Mayana said: "Grandmother, I have seen what you describe: those who settle deeply into themselves, calm and at peace, though they know they are dying. But Grandmother, this is a story about mirrors. I would like to know how it made her feel to see herself so changed?"

"I will tell you. When Felicia saw herself in the mirror, it gave her new life. She knew that she had to leave her land."

"Because she could not bear for others to see how she looked?"

"No. Because she wanted to live as the new person she had become. Now, listen:"

Felicia was a sinner—of this she was certain, for she was being punished. She wanted to atone, to convert her sorrow and suffering into faith and devotion, and what better way to seek redemption than to live the simple life of a pilgrim? She did not know how long her pilgrimage would last or where it would lead her, but she recalled that the main road leaving her village forked into another road two miles to the south that ran past by several fiefs, churches and community wells, and eventually met up with a smaller road that wound into a range of low hills, ending at a secluded monastery.

She rang for her lady's servant who sent for her minister and, when both stood before her, she disclosed to them her plan. The servant let loose a flood of tears, but promised to be loyal and to oversee the education of Clare. The minister bowed his head and assured her that he would run the fief properly in her absence. And so Felicia donned a simple dress, packed provisions of food and filled one flask with water. Then the three friends said their goodbyes. Felicia departed through the back door just before sunrise, the same door that Prudence had used months before to sneak away.

Felicia walked slowly on feeble legs, leaning heavily on a cane. Because her appearance had greatly changed, she did not fear recognition.

She was a stranger to all, and all were a stranger to her. This meant, she discovered, that she saw the people she met on the road with fresh eyes, seeing, instead of their position or role in the village or fief, seeing *them*: their soul life, their sufferings and joys as written in their eyes, in how they held themselves, in their breath and on their skin. It was a strange new kind of sight that grew more penetrating the longer she journeyed.

Most days, she would force herself to walk for hours, only pausing to rest beneath the shadow of a tree or near a community well. When evening fell, she would approach a cottage or small church. Usually, a bed and meal awaited her—hospitality for pilgrims was widely practiced. At night, she prayed, giving thanks for food and shelter. At daybreak, she prayed again, renewing her pledge to atone.

One day, she was resting by a tree when a fever befell her. She welcomed the illness. *Let the fever ravage her if this was God's will*, she thought. Her body began to slump where she sat, and beads of sweat pearled along her hairline.

She felt a hand on her shoulder. "Are you all right?" a friendly voice asked. She opened her eyes to see a young man, offering a cloth and wiping her forehead. She smiled and accepted his care.

In a glance, she studied the man, still a boy, really. The crusty skin on his hands and eyelids told her that his village had fallen for the fashion of eating bread made with flour from which the hulls were removed from the kernels, so the flour was white instead of brown and was weak of virtue. The children of such families showed a similar kind of disfigurement on their skin, or in the shape of their face or body. Another glance showed her that the boy was very thin. *He should not be traveling alone*, she thought and said, "Tell me a story, Young Man. I thirst for the sound of a kind voice. Such as yours. And I thirst for a true and good thing to be said."

His eyes opened wide, and she noted with certainty his trusting, childlike nature. Slumping beside her, he poured out his story. "We are three brothers, and my father, a Nobleman of a fief, there yonder, at the foot of the far mountains, he returned six months ago, distraught, from a meeting with the King. We went into his chamber to hear the news. He told us that the King had been counseled by the clergy. They had told the King that the farmers have become too many and must promptly be sent off to war. He said—." The boy's voice broke off.

"Go on," Felecia urged him. "I want to hear how your father heard news of the war."

"Father told us that he did not want to follow the King's orders, but that, should he refuse, our family would be cast out of the aristocracy and we would be poor."

"What were the King's orders? Tell it precisely, all the details."

"That to decrease the number of farmers, the King had decreed a war in the East. Now all able-bodied farmers must take up weapons and go off to fight.

"It nearly broke my father to tell it. For our farmers were well. Our fief prospered. The crops were abundant. Everyone had enough to eat. My father wept, saying the King had argued that once the common people are too many, and too successful, and no longer hungry, they would rise up against the King and the Noblemen, and that their revolt must be prevented with the pretense of war.

"My oldest brother listened with enthusiasm. He said that he would lead the farmers to war so he could earn great honors. He assembled the able men, old and young, and in no time they were gone.

"My second oldest brother was angry. He wanted to prove himself in battle, too, but my father would not allow it. So he stole away from the fief at night. Last we heard, he was killed in battle.

"And now, Old Woman, the farms suffer a blight and all the crops fail. My father is ill in mind and heart. No one now lives in the fief who remembers the remedies to heal the plants and restore the crops. And so I told Father that I would go out into the world and find someone to help us."

Felicia smiled gently and said, "Your journey has ended. You have found her."

"Old Woman! You?"

"Listen. Because you wiped the sweat of fever away with your cloth, and because you speak the truth, I will instruct you on how to solve the blight. Tell me exactly, all the details: when do the diseases start and how do they appear on the leaves, and at what pace do they progress on each of the vegetables and the trees?"

The boy, whose name was Karl, told Felicia about the crops and the illnesses upon them, and she, in turn, taught him all the old, traditional remedies.

"Who are you, Old Woman, that you hold such formidable knowledge?"

"I am one who is lost. I am atoning a great wrong. I cannot tell you more. But you might travel with me for a while—I believe I am headed in your direction." And she pointed with her hand—for she knew of his father and their fiefdom.

Days and weeks passed as they traveled slowly on. In Karl's company, her appetite returned. She gained strength and leaned less on her cane. Karl respected the laws of pilgrimage, and so they were mostly silent. When they did speak, it was about the diseases of plants. Felicia chided him at times for his questions, as he struggled to memorize all her answers. "Your curiosity about plant disease—it is quite unusual for a boy of noble standing."

"But don't you see, Old Woman, that I was not allowed to learn it? Father said that book reading and practical learning is a woman's work. As I have no sisters, and my mother died when I was a child, no one was there to oversee the crops when the farmers abandoned the fields to go to war."

Felicia had not considered that a young Nobleman might actually want to know such things, but that he was not allowed. She smiled then at Karl, and her eyes shone with kindness. "Of course. Ask all that you wish. My knowledge is your knowledge. I do not tire of answering your questions."

One morning, they entered a church and overheard a small assembly of townsmen and clergy. The talk was of the war's end and of vassals straggling home, mad with defeat, wielding their swords against their own people. No one was safe. Everyone now must be on the alert.

Felicia wondered if the man who had stolen her daughter had been such a soldier returning from battle, his friends and leader dead, and determined, at least, to take a wife as a prize before traveling to his own far-off fiefdom. Perhaps he'd heard a rumor about a pretty girl of the Noble class whose father was away with his men. *Yes, that could have happened.*

Kneeling in a dark corner of the church, Felicia spoke a prayer for Prudence, and then a prayer for the desolate and desperate man who had stolen her daughter. Karl, looking on from a separate pew, heard everything spoken as well. *Perhaps his brother was on his way home*, he thought, and would bring with him the farmers—those who were still alive, those who still knew the lore of plant health.

They walked on. One morning, Felicia found what she had sought: a certain fork in the road. The left way would lead through hilly terrain to the hidden monastery—the first clear destination on her uncertain journey. She embraced Karl and spoke a fond farewell. "Your way lies on the main road, but mine is in another direction. Your journey is back to the life of a Nobleman, and mine is to the life of a hermit." But Karl fell to his knees and begged her to continue the journey together. His tears wet her hands. "I feel safe and well with you, as with no other in this world.

Do not tell me to part! I do not hope to meet the men returning now, sick with war madness. I am not strong enough to stop them, or to witness their cruel deeds. It will break me."

Felecia did not know how to respond, so she agreed that Karl might accompany her to the monastery. They attempted to manage the many miles on that same day, walking at a fast pace in silence together. The road ascended into rocky hills. Heavy fog settled on the slopes in the distance. It crept down the hills until, as afternoon ebbed to dusk, it discovered the pilgrims.

Felicia and Karl walked on through the dark, cold mist, Felicia leaning heavily on her cane, while Karl supported her elbow. As exhaustion returned to her body, the old affliction of pain and loss seemed to settle on her mind as well. Felicia felt a stab, like a sword of sadness ripping through her body, bursting through her chest. Her heart missed a beat. Her knees lost their strength. She fell hard to the ground. From a great distance, she heard Karl's pleading voice, calling the Old Woman to return to him.

She had a dream: she saw soldiers stealing through the fog, swords and knives drawn. They approached a settlement of cottages. Men rushed out of their homes as the soldiers set their fields ablaze. Women and children huddled in their homes or ran for the forest. She saw the soldiers descend on them and she cried out to God, "Why must I see such a sight and have my heart broken? Of all the visions to grant a repenting soul! Do I not know what has befallen my daughter and do I not lament and pray each day?" As she wept, her heart's cry earnestly asked: Why does mayhem continue? Why are we so helpless against it?

Then the sounds of screams and clashing swords disappeared. In its place was pure, still silence. She thought, *Silence, Silence, Stillness, Gentle Living Stillness, Indescribable Gentle Silence*. Into the stillness, she could feel her despair being pulled out from her body and mind, until she was utterly emptied of it. Now her tears were of gratitude. She felt a soothing light all around. It began to warm and restore her.

She opened her eyes. In the light was the form of a woman. She spoke: "Felicia. You are weary. But you are strong, and there is something

I would ask you to do."

"Dearest Mary, Mother of God, I am Yours. Tell me what to do."

The woman of light said: "The Old Ways have been lost. We cannot prevent the turnings of time, but we can soothe some of the suffering. And for this, we need new laws. Daughter, I ask that you go, as you plan, to the monastery, but not as a pilgrim. If you go as a Noblewoman you may become an Abbot, and with time be famous and revered. You can then assert the necessity to create new laws to shield the common people from young men who have no skills except to wield weapons. You can create a new code of honor in which young men find fame by protecting the weak, rather than by fighting the weak for pleasure. But the church and King can only create these laws if the nobility agree to uphold and enforce them. Therefore, you must work together, nobility and clergy. And you are chosen, Felicia, to initiate this change. Listen closely now as these are the laws you will suggest:

"Let no Knight fight a civilian.

"Let no Knight force himself on woman or child.

"Let no Knight fight another Knight who is unarmed.

"Let no Knight do harm to any person or being, but let him protect and defend.

"And finally, Felecia, you should work toward creating schools where men may study letters, law and medicine. In this way, the men will elevate their minds above the impulses of war. They will create a better society."

Felicia awoke in Karl's arms. He cried to see her return to life. The vision was fading from Felicia's mind, but she was left with what seemed like a very good idea: she could improve the lives of people for centuries to come. She could become an Abbott and assert the need for laws to protect the people from violence. Girls would no longer fear being stolen from their homes, taken as slaves, or assaulted when traveling. And, while she was at it, she would outlaw girls from becoming pilgrims in the first place.

Ah—the thought of it! Villages could flourish without imminent fear of plunder. Young men could survive into adulthood and see their own children reach adulthood as well. And she would found schools for the brightest boys, boys like Karl. They would have something more to look forward to than war. They could set about creating a better world.

Beneath the Story Tree, Mayana sat with her eyes closed. She thought about Felicia's meeting with the woman in the fog as she waited for the story to continue. But Grandmother did not speak. As Mayana continued to consider what it would have been like to meet the woman of light, she grew aware of a feeling of warm light, all around her. Then she was filled with stillness. She opened her eyes and looked at Grandmother. In this moment, the breeze did not blow, the insects did not buzz, and the sun in the sky stood still. Seeing Grandmother's face, her calm, shining eyes, Mayana felt overwhelmed by the beauty. She suddenly knew that she wanted only this—to sit here, just so, with Grandmother, in this perfect, endless, infinitely soothing stillness.

Now Mayana noticed that all the sadness and fear she did not even know that she carried, all her unnamed ancient memories, were leaving her, as if drifting away out of her body and mind, turning into mist and dissolving into the gentle light. Her sorrow was taken from her, too—all the tears she had shed earlier in the day. She felt utterly refreshed and renewed.

Grandmother spoke. "Do you understand now?"

Mayana hesitated. "Is *She* in you, Grandmother?"

"All are in *Her*. We are given the stories, dear Mayana, to remember Her and find our way back to Her. So, quietly now. Listen."

Felicia and Karl walked on, reaching the monastery at midnight. When she rang at the gate, Felicia no longer carried her cane. Her eyes were strong and her face was calm. Her hair was white, and she looked much aged, but her face shone with a quiet, regal quality.

A girl in her teens opened the gate. The two looked at each other, calmly mustering the changes while recognizing in an instant the person, the beloved, the one given as family to cherish and love.

"Mother," said the girl, and fell to her knees, embracing Felicia's thighs and crying from the depths of her heart. Felicia leaned over and encircled her daughter's shoulders with her arms, enfolding her in tenderness.

"Let me hold you, oh, do stand, let us embrace!"

They stood with their arms wrapped about each other for what seemed like an endless moment there at the gate, and the monks gathered around, smiling and nudging each other, sharing in the gladness.

Karl stood back, watching the scene with amazement. *Who was this Old Woman?* Karl would eventually learn her identity. He would stay with Felicia through many years' time, supporting her, learning from her, becoming book-learned, plant-learned, and wise.

But what had happened to Prudence? She had worked dutifully in the monastery to earn her meals and stay. As the weeks passed, without the distraction of mirrors, she had changed. She stopped thinking about herself and her appearance. She enjoyed the responsibilities of the house and gardens. She liked to tend and care for the pilgrims who passed through, using her knowledge of medicine to aid when needed. She listened with interest as the pilgrims told their tales, coming as they did from all walks of life, each with their own story, losses, quests, and tragedies.

Slowly, Prudence had come to understand the purpose of her mother's plans for her: it was for the people, for their families, children, and children's children that her mother had pushed her to study, work, become educated and wise.

Finally, Prudence wanted nothing more than to return home. But how could she face her mother, after what she had done?

And then her mother appeared, and her eyes shone with tenderness. Prudence had felt as though she could see past her mother's form to the person within, and, in recognizing who her mother truly was, she burst into tears.

The two spent many happy days together. They spoke of many things. At last, it was decided: Prudence would return to the fief and to its management, and Felicia would remain in the monastery. She would join the church. She would work to create laws that would improve the lives of many generations.

Prudence's return was celebrated. She was honored and adorned. But now she hardly glanced at the mirrors. She had grown into a woman, she knew who she was, she knew who the woman in the mirror was, and she was grateful to take on her responsibilities.

One night, her little sister reminded her of the story she had once begun to tell. Clare said, "Can you finish it now?"

Prudence recognized the need to have a story told to its end, and so she invented a tale about a community of little men where runaways could cook and clean and live happily. She said that the evil stepmother had eventually shown up, plotting revenge against the girl.

Prudence did not know how to go on with the story. It made her sick to remember how she had maligned her mother and made up this story in the first place. So she drew it to a quick close: both the girl and stepmother found their end. The girl was poisoned, and the clan of little men pushed the elderly woman off a cliff to her death.

But Clare disagreed. She said, "That's not how it goes. The evil stepmother dies, of course, but the girl is revived by a prince who happens to ride by on a horse and is struck by her beauty. That is how such stories end, Prudence! Don't you know that?"

Prudence kissed her sister on her cheek and said, "Then let it end so."

She could not know that this very story would live on as the story of Snow White, whereas no one would remember how she and her mother had taken different paths to meet each other with eyes that saw true, and how they had devised a plan to improve the lives of the people.

Beneath the Story Tree, Grandmother asked, "Do you now understand the meaning of the Deep Mirror song?"

"I think so—when I felt her light just now, I understood that if I could always look through the surface of things to what is within us all, I would love and cherish every person and every being, because every creature is Her.

"I understand, Grandmother, that when She looks into the mirror of her own mind, she sees all of us. When we are aware of Her, when we feel Her fully, then all sadness is lifted and dissolves into Her light. But most of us do not see Her. Most of us look *at* the world, and *at* each other and do not see *She in Whom we are Held*. This kind of sight is small."

Grandmother's face lit up with her broad smile.

The way of heart—the Old Songs tell it: learn the joyous nature of self through the Grandmother Song, and the quiet, flowing and growing nature of self through Tree Grow; learn to move between the above and the below with The Tower, and finally, learn the art of true sight with the Deep Mirror song.

But what happens to those who feel the calling to practice the Old Songs, but who live in a time when no one can teach them, and when even the Grandmothers cannot recall the meanings?

The next story is about such a woman.

Ella's Calling —

Falling or Flying

Many years after Snow White and Felicia's time, a girl will be born who is named Ella. She is called Ella because, even as a baby, her features are so fine and her presence so electric that she seems to be a child of the fairy-folk. But rather than cast her out into the forest, as was the common response to such a child, the girl's mother will say, "She is a blessing. See how she shines! She is a child of joy. Let us call her Ella to remind us of her fairy-origin. But let us keep her with us, grateful for their blessing, and never fear her as a curse."

This is Ella's story. Her father, a tradesman, made a fortune selling silk. With his wealth, he bought an enormous property upon which servants and farmers toiled and hungered, as had always been their fate. A practical man, Ella's father foresaw grave danger. One never knew when hysteria might break out again among the people, and the burnings of witches begin. The birth of such a daughter brought great uncertainty. He struggled with his resolve.

"Dora," he said. "We shall keep her. The girl is our own blood-daughter. She will not bring a curse upon us. There is no such thing as fairies or witches, and even should such creatures exist, there are certainly none in our family."

Thus, Ella could stay with her parents, and she grew into a much beloved girl. Whether planting flowers in the garden, baking scones in the kitchen, or practicing stitchery with the seamstress, everything she touched was good and much admired. She herself was most beautiful, and though she surely knew it, she was not vain. She would stand by the mirror for good lengths of time, not admiring herself as much as admiring the fact that life could create such a pretty girl. One time she looked intensely into her own eyes in the mirror and thought she saw so much beauty there, beauty she could not fathom, that she reeled back in surprise. Yes, Ella was enthralled with the world and its beauty, and was intrigued to learn more about it. She liked her classes, she did well in math and book reading. She also liked to hear stories about old times, to learn fragments of ancient songs and the steps of traditional dances that were so old no one could tell her their origins. But she especially enjoyed hearing tales about fine princes who marry beautiful, virtuous, deserving girls.

When she was only nine years old, her mother died suddenly. The neighbors whispered it was punishment for keeping a child so obviously superior that she must be fairy folk. Her father defended the girl, saying anyone might die suddenly of lung illness, regardless who their daughter might be. The servants also stood by their beloved young friend. But despite the kindness shown her, Ella grew into a loner and a dreamer. She no longer paid attention to her classes, and her work in the garden and kitchen was distracted, at best.

Truth be told, she had always had a dreamer's streak. She had felt called. The calling seemed to come from the clouds, the trees, the flowers, from the glow of grass on a foggy day, from the starry night sky, and from the snow-capped mountains in the distance.

Her father eventually re-married—a worldly, kind woman whose own daughters were slightly older than Ella. Her father and new mother hoped the friendship of the older girls would stop Ella from being such a dreamer. But the new situation only made it worse. For Ella had been much attached to her mother, and this attempt to replace her only made her withdraw still more.

One servant, sensing her trouble, told her that her mother lived in the pear tree down by the well. It was, of course, a tale of fancy. But after that, Ella was often found down by the well, talking to the tree and crying. Her stepmother tried to comfort her in her grief, placing her arm about her shoulders and kissing her warmly on her cheek, but the girl resisted her affection, turning away and frowning. There was nothing her stepmother could say or do to interest the girl in her new sisters or in her

lessons. Instead, Ella spent more time with her beloved servants, especially with the one who had told her about her mother and the pear tree.

Time passed, but rather than bringing healing, a still greater grief seemed to take hold of Ella. At night, she could not bear to be close to her new family. She would curl up next to the fire in the kitchen, unmindful of her fine clothes or clean hair, and how they were dirtied by the soot and ashes on the hearth. When her stepmother tried to bring her back to bed, she would cry and kick. After several such attempts, her stepmother realized there was nothing she could do, and she gave up altogether. *Let her sleep by the fire then, the little Cinder-Ella!*

To her husband she said: "We cannot allow the child to be the ruin of our happiness. She insists on living with the servants and sleeping by the fire! I will not struggle to bring her into the family and give her an education if she does not want it."

The father nodded and said, "So be it. Let her live with the servants. When more time has passed, we will try again."

Ella worked in the fields, planting and harvesting the crops. She now lived the life of the servants—but she was mostly living in a world of her own. She often fantasized that she could feel her mother's hands in the fire's warmth, touching and stroking her back as she fell asleep. And she often heard the same soft calling from the fire that she heard in nature, as though all of life were calling out for some part of her to join it.

Years passed. Life was often hard. Sometimes Ella did not eat, for she shared the servants' lot, including their hunger. She did not find hunger to be unusual; it was just one more part of the general loss and pain that encompassed her. And when all the servants were hungry, there was tension between them but also closeness. They would go out together to gather bark from trees and herbs and mushrooms from the meadows, and then dry and ground these into a fine powder to use as food. Some of the plants were mind-altering. Then the servants would sing and dance in an ecstatic trance. Sometimes, after eating these herbs and mushrooms, she could see her mother's face in the fire. Then Ella would go down to the pear tree and talk to her mother, who would appear to her in the early dawn as a figure rising from the mist on the grass. Her mother always said the same words: that Ella was dearly loved, and that she should follow the calling of her heart.

One day, her father went out to find Ella in the fields. He spoke to her in a firm voice, saying, "We have given you time to come to terms with the loss of your mother. Now you must rejoin your family and plan your future life."

Ella did not understand, but she followed her father upstairs to a room that long before had been her own. There, the servants bathed and dressed her. She was introduced to her tutor, whose job it was to remind her of her duties as the daughter of a Noble family.

Ella did not know what was expected of her. She had only dim memories of these people. Her community was the fire, the dawn, and the straight-spoken servants. The pear tree was her greatest love. When sitting high in the tree, it seemed to her that poetry and song flowed into her mind from the leaves and branches. She climbed there as often as possible to listen.

It was soon clear that Ella remembered nothing. At dinner, the use of cutlery baffled her. She watched how the others ate and tried her best to imitate them, but the rich food and white bread turned her stomach.

She knew that she was expected to make conversation, but about matters that had never concerned her. At a loss, she said nothing, and received stern looks of disapproval from her father. Sleeping in a bed was most difficult. She felt as though suffocating in softness, so used she was to the hardness of the hearth that let her feel her bones.

Still, she did her best. She allowed the servants to wash her, dress her, and do up her hair each day. She tried to read and do her figures, and she attempted the use of a needle.

One day, a grey-bearded gentleman came to visit for mid-day supper. While they ate, he looked at her in a way that made her feel restless. After supper, he and her father went into the library and spoke for hours. When he had gone, she learned he had asked for her hand in marriage. Her father said, "He is the owner of a large rural estate that can benefit from a woman of your skills. You must accept."

Ella clenched her fists to her chest. "I will not marry him."

"You must," her father said. "This man made a fortune abroad and inherited his father's property. He has no love of societies, dinners or parties, so you will not be ill at ease. You can manage his servants. It will not be a terrible life. You will see."

That night, Ella left her bed and fled barefoot down cold stone steps to the kitchen. As she sat in a fever, before the fire, shivering and shaking, her mother's face emerged from the flames. In a clear voice, she told her daughter to go to the pear tree.

Ella thought about her beloved tree, but she was too exhausted, faint, and frail to go there. In her mind, she imagined floating light as a wisp of cloud, crossing through the kitchen and slipping out the back door. She could not feel her feet touch the ground as she dashed through the garden and fell weeping at the foot of the tree. It was a full moon. The grass was steeped in moisture. A mist of starlight-shimmering-droplets moved over the ground and gathered about her. Then the trunk of the tree leaned over protectively above her.

Again, she heard the clear voice of her mother. "Gather your courage! There will be a great dance at the King's palace this very night. The Prince will choose a bride. He will fall in love with the girl who is the purest of heart. Make ready to go!"

"But how can I go, Mother? I am not dressed, and I have no carriage."

"I can dress you!"

From the branches above, a spray of leaves cascaded to the grass beside her. They transformed into a dress of fine-woven fabric, which the girl put on.

"And here is your carriage!"

A shower of pears fell to the ground and turned into an elegant carriage, horses, and a driver.

"Now, go! All will be well!"

Cinderella stepped into the carriage and leaned back on the seat, surrendering herself to the magic. She was driven along roads she had never traveled, over icy streams and through dark forests she had never seen. She drew closer to the looming, snow-clad mountain, until she arrived at her destination and looked up: there stood the crystal palace, with high sparkling towers and radiant windows.

As she walked up the long flight of stairs, the door flew open. Standing at the threshold of a light-flooded hall, she saw, sitting at the far side, a young man who raised his eyes toward her. In this moment of eyes-meeting, the musicians did not play, the dancers did not dance, the light of the candles did not flicker. The Prince, looking ever so strong and noble, walked towards Ella, never shifting his gaze from hers. Then his lips touched her fingertips, they strode to the center of the ballroom, and the music commenced.

Before Ella could even wonder if she remembered how to dance—for the last time she'd danced, she'd been a child—the dance seemed to just come to her, as if she already knew, already anticipated and understood each twirl and dash. As they flew through the ballroom, her eyes locked with his, she felt the purist and deepest affinity, as if they had known each other forever, or as if they had starved together—for those who go through the hunger seasons together sustain one another through their closeness.

As they danced, she sensed they were leaving the floor, were rising above the crowd, dancing in mid-air, and then dancing in the clouds. *It must be my Mother's doing*, she thought. *She* can do anything. And then they danced among the stars. Ella thought only of the man in her arms. He had been calling her all her life from the clouds and the mountain and the trees. In the arms of her lover, there was no more yearning, no more calling. She was home, and she knew that in years to come, they would work together in the fields, sleep together on the hearth, and endure hard winters. They would have children, and they would teach them the Old Songs—though she wasn't sure what these songs were, she only knew fragments; it was more a feeling she had that there must be songs that were also teachings, and that it was imperative that the children learn them. And her children would visit the pear tree. They would know *Her*. All would be right.

Early next morning, the servants alerted Ella's father and stepmother that Ella had been found again before the hearth, pale and trembling, her dress soaked through with fever-sweat.

They had called her by name, shook her by the shoulders, splashed her with water and tried to stand her up, but every attempt to elicit a response had failed—for Ella's mind was elsewhere.

The doctor was called. He tried the salts and vapors, and then pronounced her insane. Her horrified father asked the doctor what they could do for her. "Let her stay where she is most comfortable," he said. "If she prefers to sleep by the fire, let her. Move her into the garden during the day if it does not cause her fear or distress. I have given her water to drink and bread softened with barley soup to chew and she has taken it, though drinking and eating did not bring her to her senses and she is still in her trance. This is the best you can do for now: Keep her alive. Feed her, clean her, and give her fresh clothes if she will allow it. Let me know if there is any change."

Over the next several months, Cinderella's state improved. She sometimes came out of her trance and seemed to see those about her. Then she would speak of the tree, dress and carriage, and of how she and the Prince were together and happy in his kingdom.

As time went on, she expressed a preference for sitting beside the pear tree. As still more time passed, she seemed to heal. Not that she came back to being her old self, but she was more aware of those around her, would address them by name and accept more willingly the food and drink they offered.

As she entered this phase, the servants noticed a change in her behavior. Rather than conveying a sense of confusion about being in two worlds at once, she seemed at peace with herself and with everything around her. The servants joined her whenever they could; they said sitting in her presence brought them happiness.

One day, Ella began teaching what she called the Old Songs, about the mirror, tower, tree, and river. When she was alone with the women, she taught them the Grandmother Song. She told them about the dance of the hands, and told them why it is important to meet the wolf and the joy of the body. She said that women often go from one task to the next, carrying responsibility for new life and community wellbeing, but without knowing who they are. She said that the calling they hear from the trees, the mountains and the clouds is their own nature, calling them to remember. And she said that her own Mother-Nature had taught her the Old Songs, and taught her that change for a better life had to start from within each woman and man. "In here," she pointed to her heart, "you learn what is real. You learn to see. To listen. You find trust, joy, and love. And in your own heart, you meet your Lover."

"And the tragedy of men," she would say when men were present, "is that they learn from earliest childhood that their purpose is to offer their lives to the King. Yet, one farmer is as worthless as the other in the King's eyes, and any man can be called to be a soldier at any moment and be away from his fields and family. But the human has two hands, the man and the woman. They must know who they are and join strengths to build a life that is worthy."

The servants now told tales of Cinderella in the village. Soon, a constant stream of people arrived in her garden from the surrounding villages and the wider countryside. They wanted to hear what she had to say, and to experience the peace she exuded.

Her parents went along with it. Her father remembered how his first wife had spoken in favor of keeping the child, despite her special aura that made the neighbors suspect she was fairy-born. Though her parents did not sit with her at the pear tree, they also did not put a stop to the unceasing arrival of visitors.

One night, Ella cried out for her father. The servants woke him. He dressed and hurried down to the hearth where he found her, huddling beneath a blanket, eyes reddened and cheeks in a fever, as if crazed again.

"Father! Go with me to the pear tree. Now! Mother says that you must come!"

Ella and her father walked to her place near the tree. He stood by and watched as she sat and closed her eyes. For a good year, he'd heard strange stories about his daughter and he did not know what to expect. He tried to stay calm. Time crawled by. He fought against his wish to lie down in the grass, close his eyes and sleep.

In the early dawn light, he thought he could see the form of a woman emerge from the tree. He saw her move to his daughter's side. As she placed her hand on Ella's head, his daughter sighed beneath the ethereal touch.

The father squinted to see more clearly—was this apparition his dead wife's ghost? Or was she someone else? His question showed in his face and as the figure gazed at him, a smile on her lips, he heard these words in his mind: "I am of the ages, and I am ageless. I am beyond being and am all beings. Find me and you find your peace."

Ella opened her eyes. She saw her father fall to his knees and cover his face with his hands. "Did you see her?" she asked. "She wanted me to bring you here."

He whispered, "I saw her," and he embraced his daughter's feet. "I am so grieved. I did not know! Did not think! Since you were a child, you have been *her* servant. Your dreaminess, your preference for the fire, for the life of the servants, and even your madness—all were your way to be close to her. I am so ashamed. To think I tried to force you to marry! My dearest Ella, I will never force you to live a life that you do not choose. You are a gift to us all."

The girl placed a hand on her father's head. She felt the finest pressure of her Mother's hands over her own, felt the forgiving, healing presence. The girl smiled. All was good.

Beneath the Story Tree, Mayana struggled to open her eyes. Just moments before, she had felt as though floating in the arms of a proud young hunter while the words "gentle, gentle, gentle" resounded in her mind. She had not wanted to leave that vision.

Grandmother sat, eyes closed, in silence. On the other side of the valley, sunlight dipped behind the shadowy mountains. Grandmother's thoughts were with the sun and the growing darkness.

Mayana said, "Grandmother, you are tired. But help me understand. Why did Ella dream the story of the Prince?"

Grandmother smiled, gently, softly. She had hoped Mayana would ask this question. *The teachings were almost complete.*

"Mayana, you told Carmona a story about a woodsman, because you are very young. The man who lives in your body and heart appeared to you as a protector. But Ella is a woman. She must meet her inner man as a lover. He is the heart of her wolf. He calls to her. He tears down the thorns around the tower where she sleeps. He kisses her awake—awake to herself."

Mayana took in Grandmother's words. Then she said, "Is this what growing up is all about, Grandmother? Do the songs lead us there?"

"It is a great part of it. But this you should know, Mayana: if Ella had befriended her wolf from the time she was a child, and if she had practiced Tree Grow and Tower, and if she had practiced seeing beyond distortion, she might have received her inner lover's kiss without leaving the common world.

"But for Ella, in the times she lives, there can be no other way. She has no traditions to prepare her for awakening. She must jump off the cliff before she can fly in order to learn how to fly. But she is called by the Mother, attuned to that calling through years spent living and working with the servants and farmers, by sleeping on the hearth before the fire, and through her meditations at the tree. Many others will long to fly, but will jump off the cliff and break on the rocks below—for they do not know how to listen to the spirit of wisdom all around them. It will always be the rare ones, like Ella, who can fly, guide, and heal."

Mayana's cheeks were wet with tears. "I see them," she said. "I see so many trying to fly. I want to reach out and help them. But I do not know how."

Grandmother's face seemed just a shadow, in the failing light. "What we can do, Mayana, is our part to do. We revive the Old Songs; we teach and pass on the entire tradition again; and in our hearts, we honor them."

Grandmother and Mayana sat beneath the Story Tree: the girl, beginning her life, but with the strength of generations in her bones; the woman, the same strength withdrawing from her.

"Grandmother, you look tired," Mayana said. "This day has been long. Let us go back to the hut."

Fahrwa, too, looked tired. He yawned, but he did not move.

"I do feel tired, Mayana. I hear night calling. Or perhaps — perhaps I hear *my calling*." Her voice trailed away. She patted Fahrwa over his ears. He raised his old eyes to look at her. She seemed to hesitate.

Mayana watched as Grandmother sat a while longer, her cheek on Fahrwa's cheek, her arm draped over his shoulders. Then Grandmother raised her eyes and met the gaze of the girl. She said: "Mayana, a great journey begins for me now."

The girl shivered. Such words were spoken in the ceremonies.

Grandmother went on, "I want nothing more, Dear One, than to lie in the nook of that bough." She stood, stretched, and walked to the tree. Fahrwa also stood, stretched, and followed beside her. Mayana, stunned and uncertain, remained sitting. But then she pushed herself up and joined them.

"Good idea, Grandmother," she said. "Rest here a while and then we can go." She helped Grandmother climb onto a wide branch. Fahrwa grumbled and pawed below at the tree's trunk, as if he also wished to climb onto a branch with Grandmother. "Go now," Grandmother said to Fahrwa, extending her hand down and stroking his forehead. "Sing for me, old Friend."

Fahrwa shook his head and yowled. He limped forward to the edge of the hill and began to whine. But as the sun slid behind the mountains, he let loose with a yowling, vowelful, howling song. Far away in the distance, Mayana heard the sounds of many wolves joining in the song. Perhaps it was so. Perhaps wolves in the lands all around knew Grandmother, and understood the meaning of Fahrwa's song. Mayana only knew for certain that Fahrwa was giving thanks, and was honoring his time with Grandmother.

He sang:

Remember back then, the snow and ice, the endless chill,
When humans knew to love us.
We loved them, too: their little ones, their elder ones, their kindness.
We hunted and lived together.
Aruuhh-aruuhh!

One family we were, for endless time, across the grassy savannahs,
Alas, aruuhh-aruuhh!
Those times are gone from their memories
And our hearts are full of sorrow,
For we loved them.

Join me wolves, far and close, and sing for Great Grandmother!
She traveled the lands, all her long life,

Telling how we are one family.

As she passes the cloak of deep memory
To the girl we know as Mayana, who,
bearing the sacred red madder cloak,
now holds humans' deep memory.

We sing the *Honor to the Wise*.
We open the way for Grandmother to fly,
To fly into Deep Black Sky!

The future is now upon us, though we shall pass beyond it.
The future is now upon us, aruuhh-aruuhh,
We shall pass beyond it.

　　Grandmother had settled herself back into the tree's nook with her
hands resting over her heart. She seemed to sleep while listening to
Fahrwa's song, but when the wolves grew quiet she murmured, "Our tree

is a wonderful mother. Look how she holds me in her arms."

Mayana answered, "She is a mother for all the people. But you... you are my special mentor. The journey you speak of will wait. You need not begin it now. I will help you back to the hut. You can rest in my bed by the fire."

Grandmother's breathing was slow. Darkness was all around. "Our stories are not just for today, Mayana," she said, slowly, pausing often. "Sit beneath a tree, any tree along your life's long journey. Remember our day of tales. Look within yourself beyond distortions. This day will come back to you, all the words and all the stories. You will be here with me again, Mayana."

The girl nodded, tears stinging in her eyes. She climbed into the tree and straddled a branch close to Grandmother, who whispered, "Help me sleep. Sing for me Deep Black Sky. But first—"

Grandmother pulled several longflower seeds from a pocket that was sewn into her dress. She put them in her mouth and closed her lips. Then she reached toward Mayana and placed a single seed in the girl's open hand.

"Follow me, Mayana. We will pass through together, for we still have work to do. Not everyone can receive the *Golden Light Song*. But you are ready to know it."

The girl slipped the seed beneath her tongue. A bitter taste spread through her mouth. The *Teacher* spoke from inside her mind, as a gentle urging –

Golden Light Song —

Frog Princess

The *Teacher* spoke from inside her mind, spoke as a gentle urging:

My eyes are your eyes—see what is real!

My ears are your ears—hear what is real!

Mayana began to drum on the bough where she sat, the rhythm of ceasing and becoming. The darkness swirled, the tree swayed. The drumming pulsed through the branches, twigs, and leaves. It shivered through the trunk and down into the earth.

Grandmother listened while Mayana sang, repeating again and again the ceremonial song:

Now here,

Now there,

Into the sky,

The deep black sky,

We wander and we fly.

Mayana's emotions streamed into the song, all her remaining sadness, fear, longing—they flowed and drained out from her body, leaving nothing behind.

The Teacher spoke from inside her: Smile for the joy of the real! Nothing has come!

Suddenly, Grandmother vanished from the branch and a girl appeared in her place. She shook her hair loose and winked at Mayana, who recognized the playful eyes. "But you're..." Mayana began to say, when the girl vanished and now in her place was the wolf. Its eyes gazed steadily, coolly, at Mayana, who laughed, overcome with mirth. "Old woman, girl, and wolf! I see it now! I cannot be fooled! I know you are one and the same!"

As the wolf faded away, Grandmother appeared with her arms held upward to the sky. As she slowly brought them down, she was holding a heavy cloak. It was dyed a deep, deep radiant red, as from a triple decoction of the madder root. Grandmother wrapped the cloak about Mayana's shoulders. Its immense weight made her feel small at first; but she soon began to feel stronger. With an unquestioned knowing of certitude, she said, "It is my *Time of Choice*, Grandmother. I choose *this*."

"Mayana, your next teaching is *Golden Light Song*."
"I have not heard it, Grandmother."

"We sing it when the cloak passes and, when needed, to lift great darkness. Listen:

> Golden Light
> On the other side
> Of Great Dark Night.
> When I see you
> All that I know
> Ceases to be.
> Nothing welcomes me in
> And I am glad.

Singing the verse, Mayana found herself within an orb of golden light. It seemed to both surround and to fill her. As she breathed the light in, she disappeared into its warm radiance, and as she released the breath, she came into new focus.

Grandmother was with her in the light, and Fahrwa, too. He wore a scarf dyed red with the madder root vine. She heard him growl as if amused. "Don't you want to be swallowed whole? You come out better than before!" Many others were also present that Mayana felt she somehow knew.

With every in- and out-breath, Mayana disappeared and reappeared. *Could this be her next teaching?* She heard Grandmother speak within her: "Whether kind or cruel, rich, poor, healthy, ill, newborn or dying, in the center of all is this light."

Mayana turned to Grandmother and asked with her eyes and her thoughts: "When I disappear, a feeling of vast nothingness fills me. It is a new way of being, and it makes me feel so glad. Is this the meaning, Grandmother?"

Grandmother's voice sounded from all around her: "When the essence of not-being clears all distortion from your mind, you can know the meaning of the Golden Light Song! Now — look!"

Grandmother motioned toward a place far away. Mayana followed her gaze. She saw a beautiful golden orb, resting near the feet of a red-haired, fair-skinned girl who was kneeling by a pond, her face in her hands. Mayana heard the girl weep and felt her fear and aloneness. She ached to help her, to be near her. She willed it to be, and then, as if touched by an unseen hand, the girl turned and saw her, standing close by in the shadow of the trees.

For a timeless moment, the breeze did not blow, the water did not flow, the insects did not buzz. Then the girl spoke to Mayana. "Who are you? How is it possible that I see you?"

"It is your sorrow and your sincere desire for guidance that have opened your sight. Who am I? Have you heard the story about a Girl in a Madder Root Cloak?"

"I am afraid I have not heard this story."

Mayana noted that the girl, nearly a woman, was dressed in a glistening gown of pearl-embedded silk, yet her dress was muddied and her hair was in disarray. Mayana said, "Have you heard the story about a girl who learned to tell the difference between a wolf and her grandmother?"

The girl's face lit up. "I have heard this tale. We call you Red Riding Hood, and your story is a warning not to take risks."

Mayana laughed. "No, I am *She who renews the Old Songs*. Let me show you."

Mayana knelt before the girl and looked into her eyes. In a timeless moment, all the stories of that day were shared: the girl saw Mayana's dreams, she walked the hill to the Tree, looked into Grandmother's eyes, studied with Rapunzel in the tower, tended the sick with Melinda, and grieved with Susanne. Then she feared with Prudence, traveled with Felicia and Karl, and danced with Ella and her prince. She understood that each of these girls had overcome some kind of shame, temptation, or obstacle to renew the Old Songs in their generation. And now she became aware of Grandmother and Wolf, standing behind Mayana, and she began to tremble. "So much is lost, so much forgotten!" she said.

Mayana, too, saw and understood: the girl's name was Elizabeth. She was the daughter of one of the wealthiest men in the lands. Her father had plans for Elizabeth, plans that were foreign to her nature. This is why Elizabeth was weeping beside the pool.

"Tell me your troubles. Let me help you," Mayana said.

Elizabeth began: "My father is a kind man, but ever since I can remember, he has held meetings at night with men he calls 'Brothers.' My mother left us when I was just a girl and I don't know where she went or why. I've often asked my father about the meetings; I've thought perhaps something about them drove Mother away. But Father has avoided my questions.

"My greatest solace, when I am troubled, when I am missing my mother, is to walk alone in the forest. I never feel more alive and at peace with myself than when I am surrounded by natural life, so I come here as often as I can.

"But now Father has declared I must be sent away and married, to forge a firm alliance with another family. When I would not agree, he brought me a present, an orb that is made of gold, heavy in the hand and beautiful in its perfection—the very orb that lies beside me now. He said, 'I ask only this: wherever you go, take it with you. Look at it. Understand what it means. It is my legacy to you, to your children and your children's children. When you have understood, you will know why you must marry the man of my choice.'

"The Brothers have been coming more often lately, and their voices are loud and sometimes brawling. Their meetings are clearly of great importance to Father, so I confronted him again.

"'You ask that I do your will, Father, but you don't explain why. Tell me, what are these meetings about? What do you discuss behind closed doors?'

"I was carrying the golden ball as I spoke, and, seeing the orb, his face softened. He told me then about our family—how we had acted as monk-knights in ancient wars and had kept safely locked away the gold of Kings.

After the war, our intentions were distorted by those who wanted the gold for themselves, and bloody revenge was enacted against us. The few of us who escaped hid our history, hid who we are, and joined the other clans. With time, we set ourselves up as noblemen and merchants across many countries. Now, my father said, the Brothers were poised to gain more influence in a changing world. It would be slow work and take generations to accomplish. He finished, saying that now I must surely understand what it is all about, and marry the man he had chosen, for, he said, bonds of blood are of highest significance.

"I felt overwhelmed by my father's disclosures and wanted to be alone, so I found my way to this pond and let everything he said pass through my mind. I've been staring at the orb and wondering, what does it mean? How is it related to the task Father asks of me? Must I marry a man I do not know or trust? Lead a life I do not understand or want? Raise my children to serve the future of the Brotherhood? Why am I part of a scheme that no one will explain to me?

"It cannot be! These men belong in a world long dead. Ancient alliances, secret plans—these cannot have a place in my life! Am I to be sold like some princess? Do I not have a right to choose my path, my destiny?

"Overcome by grief, I fell to my knees and wept. Never have I felt so alone. Never needed my mother more!

"Then a force, like an unseen hand, directed my attention to the shadows beneath the trees and I saw you—shrouded in gentlest light and wearing a red cloak. I knew you had come as an answer to my despair."

Now the two girls embraced, holding each other close. They wept as their minds probed the future, for they saw sorrow and devastation for centuries to come. They saw plans of great promise, leading to great wrong. They saw the loss of the Old Songs. The sweetness of their friendship provided the starkest contrast to the visions that oppressed them, and their hearts beat as one.

Mayana said, "Don't be afraid. You know the Old Songs now and you cannot be deceived. Look!" She took a step back and regarded the girl. "I am passing the red cloak to you!"

She sang:

Golden Light
On the other side
Of Great Dark Night.
When I see you
All that I knew
Ceases to be.
Nothing welcomes me in
And I am glad.

Amazed, Elizabeth saw herself within a golden, light-filled orb. When the vision faded, she reached for Mayana, saying, "Red Riding Hood, can you stay? Can you help me? Can you tell me what to do?"

"I can only tell you this: the golden ball at your feet is not a true orb of light. Look beyond the distortion of your mind to see what is real! Then you cannot be fooled."

Elizabeth took the heavy sphere in her hands. Its surface, catching a sunbeam falling through the trees, reflected the light with a harsh, blinding flash that made her shut her eyes and turn her head away.

Her father had wanted her to "spend time" with this orb; to "play" with it as though it were a toy. He seemed to think it would show her something that would change her mind about the marriage. But besides being heavy to hold, and reflecting the sun's light in an unbearable fashion, what could it do? How was it supposed to impress her?

She looked at the orb again. Stories of kings and kingdoms, and images of great rulers, conquerors and priests came to her mind. Some of them held 'The Orbis Terrarum,' a plain round globe that represents dominion over the world. Others held an Orb topped with a cross, the 'Globus Cruciger,' that showed the triumph of Christianity and Christian Rulers.

Could it be that simple? Was Father saying that if she married the man he chose for her, a world of riches and power would be hers and her children's? Or did he intend more? Was he saying that, like kings and popes, their family would one day "hold the world" in their hands?

For a moment, Elizabeth considered what it would be like to accept her father's proposal. She imagined a life of wealth and power, of belonging to the few who held the globe in their hands rather than being one of the many over whom the globe would rule. Did she want to forgo this promise? Surely, the welfare of her future children must be her highest priority. Perhaps she should accept her father's plans after all.

Mayana's voice, interrupting her thoughts, said, "Remember, this orb is not the true orb of golden light. Nor does this toy endow you with power from that light. It is just a bit of polished gold. No more."

Elizabeth, hearing Mayana's words, came out of the gold-trance. She saw the true nature of the orb, its lure, and temptation. She shouted then through tears of anger, "You brag, you bribe, you trick, you lie!" With a grimace of disgust, she drew back her arms and flung the oppressive thing into the water. But when she turned back, the vision of Mayana was gone.

Elizabeth walked home through the forest, all the while keeping the memory of Mayana fresh in her mind and imagining the red cloak about her shoulders. Her father was waiting for her in the Great Room by the fire. Not seeing the orb, he demanded where Elizabeth had left her toy.

"I am too old for toys, Father. And we do not live in olden times. Soon I will be an adult. Soon I can decide what I want to do with my life!"

His voice rang with anger and frustration as he said, "I trusted you to keep it safe! Do you have any idea what that ball of gold is worth?"

A loud banging at the entrance to the manor interrupted their speech. They waited in silence until a servant knocked at the door of the Great Room and then entered, followed by a man wearing the Brothers' dark garb. As the man approached, they saw that he carried the golden orb!

Averting his eyes from Elizabeth, the Brother bowed to her father and said, "Sir, I followed your daughter into the forest. There I saw her kneel by a pond. Then she rose and spoke to the air before casting the orb into the water. I waited until she left and then plunged into the pool to retrieve it—for this treasure is worth a kingdom and I deem you would be loath to lose it."

The man now turned and bowed to Elizabeth. "Your beauty and intelligence are known and esteemed by all the Brothers. I hope you will not hold my service to your father against me when I ask you to accept the promise of marriage."

Elizabeth's father felt a wave of satisfaction that his men obeyed him with such devotion, and his smoldering expression grew smug. His daughter must surely emulate their obedience and accept his decision. "Thank you. You have done well and can go now." He signed for the man to leave their presence. When the door closed, he demanded, "Elizabeth! What's this?"

Elizabeth's emotions ran high as well. "You had me followed!"

Her father held back. She had caught him out. "Indeed, Daughter. He should have met you as if by accident in the forest. He should have sought your friendship and trust. Yet you shall marry him, even now, Elizabeth, for he is a Brother, a keeper of our plans, and a good man. Because he retrieved the golden orb, we both stand in his debt."

Elizabeth scoffed. "I should marry this frog-prince who dives into the mud to retrieve your gold! A man who shows no kindness toward a girl who grieves! You meant to train me to follow your course, even to accept the man of your choice. Now you must accept that nothing has come of it!"

The air where they stood was still. The flames in the fireplace did not flicker. Neither of them took a breath.

The Great Room was her father's favorite place. It housed a library of secret books that the Brothers had sought and copied over hundreds of years, and it sheltered many examples of her father's and her grandfather's passion: intricate instruments of technology finely crafted in copper, silver and brass. The machineries stood upon large polished walnut tables. Each explored and showed a law of mechanics, chemistry or astronomy— sciences that two generations before were incipient and new, but that now would drive industries and create a new world. At the eastern wall stood an enormous fireplace; generations of men had sat there and planned the future that he and his daughter now inhabited.

Elizabeth's father broke the stillness. He motioned Elizabeth to sit with him before the fire. He was silent now, his anger flown. Instead, he seemed sad. He did not know how to address his spirited but disobedient daughter. He did not want to break her will, or scare her away, as he had her mother. And she was right. They no longer lived in an age when men could determine their wives' and daughters' choices. This was a new thing. His own mother had never dared speak so with his father, and when his own wife had challenged him, he had not listened. Now, strangely, and against his better judgment, Elizabeth's courage both delighted and frightened him. Not knowing how to proceed, he waited for Elizabeth to speak. Surely, he could persuade her about the value of his plans. Surely, she would accept the wisdom of his experience. He had been holding the orb on his lap. Now he placed it on the hearth and the light of the fire danced freely on its surface.

Elizabeth's anger also cooled, leaving her refreshed and confident. She recalled the visions she'd seen with Mayana by the pool and said, "Father, every age brings forth those who aspire to rule the world. I look at the golden orb you have given me and wonder: Do the Brothers harbor such a plan? Is this the true aim behind your secret meetings?"

Her father, stunned by her question, said, "Of course not. It is foolish to think that any one person, or any group of people, could ever rule the world. It's not possible, not by decree or by army. But, of course, you understand that members of our Brotherhood are in high places in every country. And we count on our beloved wives and daughters to stand by our sides."

At first, Elizabeth thought his answer was reasonable. But then a voice inside her mind said, See what is real! The Brothers keep their plans secret from their wives and daughters. Why? Is it because if the women knew what was hidden from them, they would never agree?

Choking back her tears, Elizabeth said, "Father, hear me out. At the forest pool, I had a vision. I saw not this cold heavy ball you gave me, but an orb of actual light, and in this place of light I met a girl, and she showed me . . . I saw . . . ."

"Calm yourself, Elizabeth. You are becoming hysterical!"

Sobbing, she said, "I saw the loss of so much!"

Seeing his daughter in distress, and remembering the last time he spoke with his wife, her Father reached out and put his arm around Elizabeth's shoulders. Elizabeth felt her father's touch and knew he would not push her away. He was listening.

"There is a power, Father, in this place of light. It does not wish to influence kings and popes, or to start wars, build industries, create a new world—like you do!"

"But you are mistaken! Such is not our goal, Elizabeth!"

"I know you will not share with me your plans. You would rather die than confess it. You've probably sworn to do so! But there is something you need to know, Father, that we all need to know . . . ."

Tears started in her father's eyes as he recalled his wife speaking words similar to these. He hadn't listened then, and he had lost her. He forced himself to focus on his daughter.

Elizabeth continued, "I see what the world is like. I see what has happened in the past and what is happening now. Do not think I do not know. I see how factories have replaced family farms and village stores, and how men of greed and status prosper at the cost of the common man. Good and honest workers have lost their independence. To survive, they work long hours under conditions that make them ill.

"I see with horror how children, too young, too poor, are made to work in dangerous conditions; how the boys turn to alcohol and crime, and the girls to prostitution.

"I have read of distant lands that are plundered and corrupted. In the East, addiction to cocaine was fostered to serve the interest of those who would oppress their lands.

"In the African Trade, men and women and children are enslaved and sold.

"I see, too, how the priests of a rich and powerful Church use their teachings to whip people into obedience and submission to their will, calling it the Will of God."

Her father's eyes viewed her steadily now, as if preparing for whatever she would next say. He had arranged for her a fine education, but he hadn't expected that her schooling would be used against him. He said, "Enough incrimination. You and I know these things well."

Elizabeth gestured to the machines on the tables. "I know how you think. You believe you are cleverer than others, that you are discovering how things work so you can make them work for you. But just because you have invented fancy toys does not mean that you are any closer to solving the genuine mysteries of life than people who lived thousands of years ago. Father, not until we know who we are can people live with benevolence. If we take the wrong route forward, we only grow farther from true solutions. To think, as you do, that machines make us more advanced—

"I saw the solution in the light, Father. We find it in life itself. In the food, the water, the air, the beauty of the earth. We find it in the health of a child, in the love of a spouse and parent. We see it in the minds of men and women when they live together in balance, one hand helping the other. There is an ancient system of knowledge, Father. It is bound up with the body, is a code that we can decipher from our oldest stories and songs, and can re-invent for our times."

Elizabeth, her face calm now, continued to tell her father what she had learned with Mayana in the shadows and the light. And her father continued to listen.

Finally, he shook his head and said, "Even should what you say be true, it is too late. Nothing will come of it. We cannot change the consequences of the course that we have followed for centuries. It is as you say. We have conceived a new order to the world's unfolding. We cannot undo what our forefathers have done. We cannot change the direction of their plans. We might hope that all our past wrong turnings come together for good in a far future time. But, Daughter, if our doings should somehow work to good, it will be no thanks to us. I know that now."

Feeling her father's despair, Elizabeth took his hand and said, "I have learned a song to lift great darkness." And she sang:

Golden Light
On the other side
Of Great Dark Night
When I see you
I cease to be
Nothing takes my place
And I am glad

Elizabeth and her father found themselves within an orb of light. Elizabeth, overjoyed to once more see Mayana, Grandmother, and Wolf, joyfully embraced them. Then she turned to her stunned father, who stood with tears streaming down his face. "Do you see, Father? All that we thought we knew has flown! Beyond all doings and plans is an endless beginning, is light, is knowing who we are. Even those who despoil the earth and ruin humankind discover their nature here—and can begin again."

Father opened his hands and reached for the light that he felt and saw all around him. "I can't hold on to it! I can't keep it for myself! It is

140

given to me freely, and yet there is no end to it! Why didn't I know?

"Daughter, I see now what it is all about!" he said. "The priests call this renewal—a new start because we feel altogether new, altogether known, welcomed, upheld, forgiven. Loved. Able to love others. To love you, Elizabeth. And your mother."

Elizabeth and her father moved close together. "I feel your love," she said. "This is how we are meant to be—is what religions could teach, yet most do not understand. But Father, tell me, what are you going to do with the golden ball?"

She pointed through the light to the orb, glittering on the hearth in the firelight. He turned to look as well, and as he did, she and her father were again standing in the Great Room.

"I don't need it anymore," he said and shunted the orb into the fire with his boot. "It is just a symbol of a reality that I previously imagined, but now I understand. It is as if the opposite of everything I believed before is true. Do you know—all your life, Elizabeth, I thought that my passing the globe to you would be the end of my journey and my purpose.

But it was your purpose to show me where my true journey begins. And as for such things as this orb," he gestured toward the fire, "it is clear to me now that owning such things is less important than giving them up when the time requires."

Father and Elizabeth held each other's hands and stood facing one another with new recognition. "It is not what we plan for, Daughter, but what we stand for that brings down God's providence. You and I stand together for the people. This must be our promise."

Elizabeth sighed with relief and resolve. "Father, so be it. This is my choice, too."

Mayana sat again on the bough of the Story Tree. She sang for all the girls, women, men and boys that she had befriended on that long day of tales. She sang for all the children: she knew all their names, knew their fates. Then she sang Deep Black Sky for Grandmother, but with new words and meaning:

> Within the Mirror,
> Our Loved Ones all appear
> And Heart's great pain dissolves.
> Through Joy of Carrying On —
> We wander and we fly —
> How we live, how we die —

As the sun slowed its ascension, the birds hushed their chorus, and the breeze all around grew still, Mayana watched Grandmother's chest rise and fall in tiniest motions. Touching her mentor's shoulder, she could feel her grandmother's presence, just beneath the skin. Then she heard a soft hum, and knew that Grandmother was intoning her breaths.

"Grandmother, it is your time. The whole world is waiting for you to fly!"

She felt Grandmother's presence lift as a burst of gentlest light and spread into the branches of the tree. She raised her eyes to the blue beyond, following Grandmother's flight into the sky.

"I will carry it on," she whispered to the Day and the Tree. "Gladly, I carry it on."

The sun resumed its journey, the breeze flew through the leaves, and the birds took up their song. The girl listened once more as all the tales that Grandmother told were whispered through the leaves and branches. She thought about the cloak, about the color of the red madder root, and about the honor of the task she had received and the choice she had taken. And so Mayana would go on to learn all the Old Songs from the Grandmothers of her clan, and to teach them in full to the children. Therefore, wisdom and good medicine lived on for her people, many generations more.

Afterword — Hilary Jacobson, 2022

In writing this book, I wanted to present key parts of women's history that are easily forgotten or overlooked, especially the witch burnings, the suppression of women's medicine, and the role that the Catholic Church and patriarchal systems of law played in this tragedy. This history still affects women's health and experience-of-self today.

I also present my hope for a human culture in which girls are gently and playfully introduced to the powers of the female body and mind in a way that allows them to develop fully, without force or coercion, all aspects of themselves. As well, I present my hope for a culture that understands and appreciates the differences between men and women, as well as honoring all gender identities, and that enjoys the challenge of learning to live in balance, creatively and productively, with one another.

I hope to have created a work of fiction that describes the value of spiritual and transcendent experience for our sense of whole self, including our empathetic connection to animals, plants, and to each other. I include "near-death experiences" and "shared death experiences" as the climax of these tales. Humans have written about and shared these experiences throughout time and in all cultures.

In describing a Female Deity, I call on medieval accounts of meetings with "goddesses," usually at a well, near streams or rivers, or in fog. *She in the Mirror* is a reference to pre-Hindu mythology.

I intentionally include the use of plant hallucinogens, under the guidance of a wise person, as part of the human maturation process, (in our culture, we typically use alcohol, with often tragic consequences).

Finally, I attempt to describe deep experiences of meditation and to interweave them into the narration of the tales. In some of these experiences, the heaviness of the body, mind and emotion can be transmutated, leaving one feeling at once empty and full: empty of one's old self and full of something new and unexpected. Because the new state at first evades identification by the thinking mind, it is often experienced as being "nothing."

According to cross-cultural spiritual experience, interacting on a meditative level with "nothing," or "no-mind," leads to a sense of renewal and rejuvenation—as well as to other beautiful "r" words such as rebirth, restoration and regeneration, and to an embodied feeling of compassion toward oneself and others.

Once again, I thank all those who supported my writing of this book, especially Dana Williams and my son Immanuel.

If you would like to follow me, my newsletter is here: HilaryJacobson.com/sign-up

About the Authors

Dana Williams is a lifelong student of spiritual meditation, an intuitive counselor, and the author of several books on meditation.

More information: rosewaymeditation.com

Books:

- The Lord's Prayer, the Seven Chakras, the Twelve Life Paths
- Through the Doors of Perception to Heaven with the Rose Way Meditation
- Math by Grace
- Red Madder Root, Tales of Initiation (co-author)

Hilary Jacobson is the author of several books on maternal health. Her special interest is the history of women's medicine and the encoded references to plant-medicine in world mythology and fairytale. A holistic lactation consultant, she teaches and speaks internationally on her areas of knowledge.

More information: hilaryjacobson.com

Books:

- Mother Food: A Breastfeeding Diet Guide with Lactogenic Food and Herbs
- Healing Breastfeeding Grief: how mothers feel and heal when breastfeeding does not go as hoped
- A Mother's Garden of Galactagogues: growing and using milk-enhancing herbs and foods.
- Red Madder Root, Tales of Initiation (main author)

Made in United States
North Haven, CT
13 March 2024

49920667R00088